WALK
A
ROCKY
ROAD

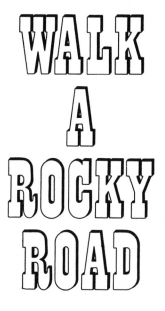

WALK A ROCKY ROAD

Mildred Lawrence

HARCOURT BRACE JOVANOVICH, INC.

NEW YORK

ISBN 0-15-294505-9
Library of Congress Catalog Card Number: 73-161387
Printed in the United States of America

B C D E F G H I J

WALK
A
ROCKY
ROAD

"First day back to school and out on a limb already!" Silvy, coming home a heap sadder than when she went, stared through the smeary window of the school bus as it wound around the curves of the blue-hazed mountains. "How in the world did I do it so quick?" She knew good and well how she had done it—pride, partly, and dreaming for a minute that she could do anything anybody else could. "Well, open mouth, empty mind!"

Miss Henderson, the new teacher, had probably thought it was a good way to settle everybody down, having them all stand up in front of the class and say what they were planning to do after they graduated next June. It was just Silvy's bad luck that she had been called on right after a lot of town kids, all full of talk about going to college way off somewhere or entering the space program or some such. Especially there had been Jan Colby, who looked like the girls on TV with their casual clothes (the Now Look) and their carefully careless hairdos (Windswept Spray for Town and Beach).

"I might be an airline hostess," Jan had said in an off-hand voice, as though that was the most ordinary thing in the world.

After that, not to be outdone, Silvy had spoken up loud and clear before she could stop herself: "I'm going to college and study to be a teacher."

She was a lot too proud to say what was bound to be the gospel truth, that she'd be staying home and helping Ma and Granny make quilts and cornhusk dolls to peddle to the tourists and collecting mistletoe and galax leaves with Pa for Christmastime. After a sufficiency of that, she'd get married young, same as her older sister, Arvilla, who had three young'uns already and kept saying, "Silvy, don't you get trapped, now! Get out of this place however you can!"

On that subject, Silvy never paid her much mind. It'd be sure-enough nice to see some other parts of the world, but it'd be scary, too, going somewhere where she didn't know people's ways, which were mighty different from her own if she could believe what she saw on the TV Pa had managed to buy last year.

The bus lurched over a broken place in the pavement, and Silvy grabbed at the stack of schoolbooks that kept trying to slide off her lap. All the way home, she hadn't said a word to anybody except Addie May Wilkins, who was sitting alongside, and very few to her, but a little thing like that never stopped Lud Bickett, gabby as usual.

"Teacher, I ain't done my homework. You gonna send me to the office?"

Silvy gave him what she hoped was a chilling glance, though Lud was a hard one to chill. Fat chance she had of ever getting to be a teacher—or anything else much either, as far as she could see.

"She had to say something, didn't she?" Addie May leaped to Silvy's defense. "What'd you have said, loudmouth?"

"I'd a-said I was gonna be a blockader," Lud went on. "That outlander wouldn't even know what I meant."

Silvy didn't bother listening to him and Addie May, wrangling back and forth the way they always did. Mood music was all it was, like on TV. In a minute now she'd be home in Curiosity Cove, which Granny said was so deep in the hills that a body had to wipe off the shadows to see the way to the stove of a morning. The cove was a far piece back, all right, but a hard-surface road went by now at the foot of the rocky lane. It was handy for the school bus and the folks that came to look at the mountains, and for getting the fifteen miles into town in case Pa's old car ever took a notion to go that far.

The bus slowed, and Lud, still talking, got off.

"Quiet here, ain't it?" Addie May said, good and loud so Lud would hear as the bus door folded shut behind him.

It would stay quiet, too, because Kel McLeod, the only one left on the bus besides Silvy and Addie May, hardly ever said anything. Likely he had the right idea, too. The trouble with words was that once a person had said them, they stayed said—not like the sentences that the teacher wrote on the blackboard and then wiped off again when she had finished with them. Silvy sighed. There was just no erasing what she had said.

She must have been touched in the head even to mention college, and she didn't know if she wanted to be a teacher anyway. It took a sight of learning that Silvy didn't have and likely couldn't get if she studied a thousand years. It'd be a way out of here, though, if she ever made up her mind she wanted to go.

"There's no future here, kid." That had been her brother Bobby, home on leave from the Army a couple of years back.

There hadn't turned out to be any future for Bobby either, catching a sniper's bullet off some place that Silvy couldn't even pronounce the name of. Anyway, he'd seen something besides a bunch of mountains and a slope covered with flame azalea, pretty as it was in the springtime.

Addie May was still going on about Lud.

"A blockader!" she muttered in Silvy's ear. "Runs in the family. His Uncle Ab had a moonshine still back in one of the hollows last year, but the revenuers got him."

Everybody knew this but hardly ever mentioned it. Some folks made blockade liquor, which was their own business, not Silvy's. Her business was trying to work out whether to cut loose from here and get a good look at life the way it was on the outside. Going into town to school every day didn't really count because every day she came back home again, out of one century and back into another, according to a magazine article she had read at school the year before.

"The southern highlanders stand on the jumping-off place from yesterday into tomorrow," was what the piece had said—which was likely true enough. Trouble was, yesterday was good solid ground under Silvy's feet, but this tomorrow looked more like hopping off a cliff into a mess of morning fog.

"Everybody out! End of the line!"

The bus driver, who was Addie May's Cousin Juny from down on Bear Creek, said the same thing every single afternoon, and he was mighty right, too, in more ways than one.

Addie May and Kel and Silvy climbed down all in a bunch alongside the little cabin that Pa, grumbling, had made for Ma the year before as a tourist stand.

"You could leave the bark on the logs," Ma had said. "It'd be a heap sight easier, and the tourist folks would think it was real old-timey."

"That ain't no fittin' way to build," Pa had said, stubborn as a six-legged mule—which was why the little building was made of split logs with dove-tailed joints all thus-and-so at the corners.

"This cabin must be mighty old," one of the tourists had said once when he honked Pa down from the house to buy some sourwood honey.

"Fifty years and six months, I figure it," Pa said, "counting the fifty years it took the trees to grow."

"See you tomorrow!" Addie May yelled at Cousin Juny, who was wheeling the bus around in the middle of the road.

Kel, with a foot-high stack of books, bobbed his head in the girls' direction and scuffed off cross-country, staring at the ground.

"What's he looking at?" Addie May wondered for the umpteenth time. "Dirt and rocks is all."

"Watching so he doesn't step on a snake, I'd say."

Silvy didn't care what Kel McLeod was looking at, if anything. It could be he was just thinking, which Silvy ought to be doing, too, if she had the brains for it, which some days she doubted. Kel picked up a stone or something, looked at it, and shied it away.

"Don't you fret yourself about Lud," said Addie May, lingering. "He don't mean a thing in the world."

"Lud? Oh, that. Who cares?"

She had nigh forgotten Lud's kidding her about planning to be a teacher. For one thing, she wasn't going to be, eleven chances out of ten, and for another, that was just the way Lud was, always setting his tongue going and letting it ramble.

"Fact is," said Addie May, "I think he kind of likes you."

Any time Lud Bickett came hanging around Silvy, it'd be the end of the world, or nearly, for somebody, Pa being of the opinion that Lud was purely useless.

"Well, thanks," was all Silvy said.

Addie May was good, always standing up for Silvy, who couldn't help looking helpless, though she hoped maybe she wasn't, entirely. It was troublesome being little and so fair and delicate-looking that Granny, who was there for Silvy's birthing, had talked Ma into naming her Silverbell, after a flowering tree that covered the woodland slopes in the spring with drifts of white tinged with the palest pink. Granny was great for everything that grew up and down the mountainside—trees, flowers, bushes, useful or handsome or some of both.

"And every bit free," she kept telling Silvy. "All them pretties just for the looking."

Or picking, in case of need. Granny knew where all the medicinal herbs grew and was always brewing up concoctions to cure a cold or a fever or a headache.

"Silvy, seeing you're just a-ponderin' and noways busy," she'd be saying any day now as Silvy was doing her homework, "run on up to the ridge yonder and fetch me a few grasps of sourwood sprouts. I can see 'em from here —pretty nigh the first to get red in the fall."

Silvy knew that as well as Granny did, from tagging behind her all these years to help tote back whatever she took a notion to gather or transplant. Silvy knew where there were seven kinds of trillium, the ghost flower with its pipe-shaped blossoms that the Indians made eye lotion out of, and even ramp, a wild leek like an onion only eight times more so. And what good would that kind of knowing do her out in the wide world somewhere—in case she ever got there?

"You didn't mean it, about being a teacher?" Addie May asked.

"I said it," Silvy said slowly, "and I wish I hadn't."

Pa said if a man said something was so, he had to make it so if it was anyway possible—not that everybody in the world held to that notion, most likely. Mountain people, though— Silvy'd never be able to hold up her head around here if she didn't keep to her word. It could be that Pa wouldn't ever hear about her crazy talk if Kel and Addie May and Lud Bickett kept their mouths closed. But even so, Silvy wouldn't feel any easier in her own mind, which was all stirred up right now like the big clouds that boiled around the mountains when a summer thunderstorm foamed up out of a clear sky.

"Never you mind," said Addie May. "You don't have to do what you don't want."

"I guess not."

Addie May wasn't ambitious or dissatisfied either. Once she graduated, she'd step out and get herself a job as a carhop at the drive-in in town and like it fine. Silvy wasn't expecting to be anybody great and important, but right now she was mighty unsettled about herself.

Addie May headed for home up the opposite slope. Kel, still studying the ground, though there was a whole mountainside starting to show color if he was of a mind to look up, had gone on by the turnoff to his house and was going on a piece further, maybe to Clate Fowler's.

Rock Shop and Lapidary, the sign said over Clate's front porch. Clate polished and peddled rocks for a living and sometimes cut sparkles in some of the bigger ones on one of his machines. Clate was real educated on the subject, Granny said—educated by himself and a hundred books. In the summertime cars from away were likely to be lined up in front of Clate's place—rock hounds, picking over the stones he had collected.

"More people fancy rocks than do quilts, seems like," Ma sometimes complained. "Well, hit's his livin', though seems he might be runnin' shy of rocks, now that he can't get around so good with that hip of his'n."

Clate had taken a fall early in the summer, down by one of the old abandoned mines, and was still hobbling around, peaked as could be. Ma sometimes carried him a blueberry pie or a batch of corn cakes, him being a lone man with nobody to do for him, and far-off kin of Pa's besides.

"Silverbell?"

Granny, with a needle in her hand, stuck her head out of the little cabin, with *Mountain Crafts* painted crooked on the sign—not that Ma and Granny managed anything real fancy. Mostly it was just quilts and a few pairs of knitted mittens and, naturally, the cornhusk dolls, dressed in sunbonnets and sometimes long cotton dresses like the one Granny had on now. Pa made chairs—straight ones with rush seats—and once in a while, when the mood was on him, a dulcimer. That was sure to get fetched away the minute Ma set it out, mostly by the people from the Mountain Guild to put in one of their own craft shops along the parkway.

"I put a face on this'n like yourn." Granny held up one of the cornhusk dolls. "And fixed her a dress outen that calico from your Sunday dress."

"It's not calico, it's—"

Silvy held her tongue. To Granny anything that wasn't silk or linen was calico.

"Can't hardly tell it from me." Silvy looked admiringly at the doll, with its painted-on blue eyes and pale yellow hair. "You aimin' to sell your own grandbaby to some outlander?"

Silvy tried to remember to talk bookish when she was at

school, but sure as anything, she dropped back into the mountain ways the minute the bus hit the road for home.

"I could get maybe fifty cents more." Granny had a spunky way of talking, to match the snap in her black eyes. "Purty little yaller-headed girls is scurce around here." She put the doll down on the counter with half a dozen others. "You aimin' to set and ponder over them books now?"

That meant, was she going to mind the shop in case of any tourists, though it was September already and the middle of the week besides.

"Nobody's been," said Granny. "Some big car stopped up by Clate Fowler's and come back a-flyin'. Was that Kel McLeod headin' up yonder, too?"

Granny didn't miss much—seemed she could mind whatever she was doing and still not let a hound dog pass by without her wondering where it was going.

"Could be." Silvy barely glanced at Kel's tall, lanky figure. "Wherever it is, he'll trip over a mountain one of these times, on account of not looking beyond his big toe."

"He's a thoughty one, I shouldn't wonder."

Granny stumped off up the lane toward the home place, a collection of gray shadows behind a screen of tulip trees, locust and redbud, mixed in with a snarl of hobblebush and devil's walking stick. The onliest things that showed much from down by the road were the tip of the TV antenna and a curl of smoke from Ma's cookstove.

Silvy laid her books down on the counter that Pa had rigged up out of a couple of chunks of log set on end with a long board stretched between. She had homework, a little, but she wasn't of a mind to do it right now. A car drove up with a couple of womenfolks in it.

"Anybody here?" one of them called.

Silvy stepped outside.

"Will you light, ma'am? We've got cornhusk dolls and a

new quilt that Granny and Ma made—Bear Track pattern—and two of Pa's chairs and some jars of sourwood honey," said Silvy, all in one breath.

"We need directions, please, to the—"

"Could we—" the other woman cut in. "I've been wanting to see the inside of one of the mountain cabins and—"

"You're welcome to step inside, but up yonder's where we live." Silvy pointed vaguely in several directions at once. It wasn't fitting to turn a stranger away from the door, but if the stranger couldn't figure out where the door was— "This wouldn't hardly be big enough."

The woman nodded. "I expect you have a big family."

This was a snoopy one, sure enough, likely full of notions she'd picked up about mountain people. Silvy's lips twitched.

"I'd have to figure." Solemn as an owl, she counted on her fingers. "Two and two is four, and then there's—" Her lips moved silently. "Seventeen, I make it, not counting Granny and Pa and Ma."

"Nineteen." Silvy jumped as Addie May showed up at her elbow. "You forgot this year's twins."

The women made tch-tching noises at each other like wrens jawing the cat.

"I see you have TV way out here," one of them said.

Nineteen kids, poverty poor, and with a TV antenna sticking up above the trees—Silvy could practically hear the two of them clucking away all the way home to Ohio or wherever it was.

"Coulda got color TV," Addie May said mournfully, "if the revenuers hadn't a-got here, with that last batch of moonshine not near ready."

Ma would be wild if she heard this string of whoppers they were telling, but people that nosed into what didn't concern them couldn't expect to hear anything sensible. Silvy could feel herself turning red in the face, half from feeling ashamed of herself and half from wanting to laugh so bad.

"Did you bring home your reading book?" Addie May never did know when to stop. "Ma wants the loan of a few pages to start the fire with."

"Help yourself," Silvy said hospitably. "Best if you don't take out of the first chapter—s'posed to read that in case I git to school tomorrow." She turned serenely to the visitors. "You were wantin' to know the way to—"

"The lapidary shop," the driver said. "That means—uh—where stones are polished and cut."

"So that's what that big word means on the sign," Addie May said admiringly. "Many's the time we've wondered."

"Half a mile straight ahead on the left," said Silvy, abandoning make-believe. "Clate Fowler's. You can't miss it."

Addie May grinned after the departing women.

"Send 'em home happy!" she said airily. "They'll be talking for a month."

More than likely they had had their minds all made up before they came—shiftless mountaineers, moonshine whisky, a big family of ragged children probably starving to death on account of the payments on the TV.

"I liked the part about using the book to start the fire," Silvy said.

All the same, she shouldn't have let the visitors upset her. She might have managed to sell them something if she hadn't let her feelings get the best of her. It wasn't the women's fault that they didn't know what was the truth and what wasn't. Likely Silvy wouldn't know a whole lot more if she was off in a new place somewhere talking to people she'd never seen before. One thing, though, she wouldn't ask questions that weren't any of her business. The thing to do would be to watch and listen and say as little as possible.

"It was the math assignment I came after," said Addie May. "Seems I left my notebook at school."

Ma gave a yoo-hoo from up at the house to tell Silvy it was eating time. Silvy took the honey jars in from the bee gums beside the road and snapped the padlock on the door. Nobody from around here would touch anything, but a person never knew who might be driving by on the road —not that the light-fingered type would be real taken with cornhusk dolls and an old-fashioned quilt or two.

If it weren't for the tourists, Ma and Pa and Granny could never even pick up tax money with all these things that came from a long way back when folks made their own or did without. "Quaint," people called them, but Silvy wondered sometimes what was going to happen when quaint went out of style?

Trudging up the lane with her stack of books, Silvy wished Pa had stayed out at the feldspar plant long enough to do more than pay for the TV and buy a battery that was supposed to keep the old car running but didn't do it. Pa wasn't lazy. He worked from "kin to cain't"—first daylight until it was too dark to see—scratching out a place for corn on his straight-up fields or making his chairs careful as could be with green wood for the legs so they'd tighten as they dried and lock the rungs in place without a single nail to hold them. The onliest reason he'd quit at the plant was it was hog-killing time, and, besides, the foreman ordered him around instead of asking polite for his help the way anybody should.

"I'm here."

Silvy put her books down on the table in the kitchen, which smelled of corn bread and some of Ma's pole beans that had been boiling all afternoon with a chunk of cured meat for flavor. One thing, they wouldn't starve right away even if cash money disappeared completely. Meal, meat, honey, vegetables, and milk—it was all a person needed to keep the body together. The soul was another thing, at least as far as Silvy was concerned. That brought her back again to what had been fretting her on the way home—not that fretting was going to get her anywhere.

Ma turned from the old cookstove, where she was dishing up. Ma was handsome in her own way—tall, straight, and plain, like a winter tree with the branches sharp against the sky. Lots of times Silvy wished she was like her instead of being so little and wispy.

"Anybody stop?" Ma asked.

"Just some women wanted to know how to get to Clate's," said Silvy, feeling guilty. If it hadn't been for the play-acting she and Addie May had put on— "Where's Pa?"

Not where she'd halfway expected him to be, in the shed off the kitchen that he'd made into a shop where he could work on his chairs and dulcimers even in cold weather. Once in a while, when he and Ma would get a giddy streak on, they'd sing to the music of the old dulcimer that he never would sell, though the Guild woman had practically gotten down on her knees begging for it.

"This'n's not for sale," he had said, stroking the rosy cherrywood. His eye had caught Ma's. "I could make you a twin to it, though, if you're in no big rush."

"Hold the door, Silvy!" She ran to the back door to let Pa in out of the dusky dark with a slab of wood on his shoulder. "Pesky Guild woman still won't let me be." He put the wood in the shop. "Fair piece of cherry, for a change."

"Pa," Silvy began impulsively, "do you think—"

But even imagining that Pa could find a way for her to go on to college was as silly as trying to fly over the mountain on the tail of a kite. If it wasn't for having said that about being a teacher right out in front of everybody, she would never have given it a thought, "impossible" being something she'd tangled with before.

Pa, not much for idle talk anyway, didn't answer, not

having been asked anything. He just sat down and waited for Ma and Granny to set his food in front of him.

"Saw a bear in back of the wood lot," he said when he had finished. "Set the dogs a-hollerin'."

Something was setting them to hollering now—Bugle, Bet, and old Blue.

"That bear wouldn't be plannin' on fresh hog for supper now, would he?"

Pa got up fast, picked his rifle off the rack, and tore outside. Silvy peered out along the lane of light streaming from the open door. Corncrib, pigpen, shed, barn—nothing moved in the shadows, but somewhere back of the corncrib there was an almighty crash, then a crackling of underbrush, as though a herd of wild pigs was trampling through, and black silence.

"Pa?" Silvy quavered. "Pa, are you all right?"

"Varmint got away," Pa yelled. "Fetch me out the lantern."

Ma lit it and carried it outside to him, with Silvy and Granny at her heels. Ma wasn't afraid of anything, but Silvy was.

"Made enough racket to wake the dead." Pa held the lantern high, a golden glow in the darkness. "That bear come back, most likely, or a wild boar. Dogs druv it off before it could git whatever it come for."

The dogs, who hadn't followed their quarry far, came straggling back, tails down, looking humiliated. Pa gave them a disgusted glance.

"Sorry lot you are!" he said. "Strong on the noise, weak on the catchin'."

They slunk away under the front porch.

"Bear," Pa decided. "Look yonder where he was turning over rocks to look for bugs. Funny time of day for it, though, black night."

"The crash?" Silvy asked. "What was that?"

Pa jerked a thumb toward the plow, tipped over on its side in a tangle with the pig bucket and the hand cultivator that Pa used to weed his corn.

"Mistook his way. Bears' eyesight's weak even by day." He held the lantern closer to a couple of tracks in the dust. "Unlikely type bear. It's mighty seldom they wear shoes."

Silvy shivered.

"Who—"

"Some feller takin' a shortcut. Didn't take nothin' else. Stranger or he'd a-sung out."

A shortcut from where to where? Strangers didn't go for walks around the hills at night, and no highlander would have gotten lost and fallen over a mess of field tools besides. Could it have been a bear after all on account of the turned-over rocks or was it a man on account of the shoes? One chasing the other maybe, though it was funny the man left tracks and the bear didn't.

"Flyin' bear, walkin' man," she muttered to Granny, picturing a bear hovering like a hummingbird while he turned rocks over with his nose.

On the whole, Silvy preferred bears because she knew what they were after—honey, pigs, food in general. Men, though—there Silvy was stopped. She couldn't imagine a thing in the world anybody'd want around here, nothing being the onliest thing there was plenty of.

"Blockader, I wouldn't wonder," Pa said, "aimin' to toll the revenuers away from his still."

Pa and lots of others, Lud Bickett included, used the old name for moonshiners, brought from across the water a long time back when the Irish used to run the English blockade with their product. So Granny said, and Granny was as curious as a cat about the whys and wherefores of things.

Silvy went back inside, spread her books out on the kitchen table, and turned on the TV. This time it was a program on what the announcer called "poverty pockets," featuring some dirty-faced kids and hopeless-looking men.

"That's those Haggises over to Deer Creek." Granny sniffed. "Triflin'est folks for miles around. Any fool can make soap to clean themselves up."

Maybe any fool couldn't if he'd never been taught. Besides, jobs were close to impossible to come by if a man didn't have training, now that everything was so technical every place.

"This is how life is in the ghettoes of the cities," the commentator said, "in the Appalachian Mountains, in the—"

"Turn that thing off!" Pa growled. "Didn't pay my good money to set and be insulted in my own house."

"He didn't mean you," Silvy said. "There's shiftless folks all over."

And poor, too, through no fault of their own. The world had gone off and left a lot of them standing, with no way to catch up. The government was trying to figure out something for all the men that didn't have jobs any more, but it took time to teach folks new ways of doing things.

There was no point in arguing about that, though. Pa, who had been around these mountains all his life and his folks before him, looking for roving room, wasn't about to let a bunch of government people tell him how he was supposed to make his way. He had his full share of pride and some extra, just like Silvy, with her biggety talk about college and schoolteaching.

She hadn't fooled anybody, she found out as soon as she slid into her seat at school the next day.

"This year," said Miss Henderson, "we're going to try

something new. A group of you will spend most of your time on the general subject of Appalachian Studies, with the idea of developing a well-rounded picture of every phase of life in this area." She smiled. "It will be an education for me, too, as this part of the country is new to me."

Silvy, remembering the lady tourists of the day before, looked under her eyelashes at Addie May. Two rows over, Lud was silently mouthing the word "outlander."

"You may each choose your own special area of study," Miss Henderson went on, "and concentrate on that for the whole year. We are going to reduce the size of the class to include only those who, we think, will be especially expert in this study."

The others were being transferred—the ones, like Jan Colby, who had the best chance of going away from here, Silvy noticed with a flash of resentment. Kel and Lud were to do the special studies, of course, and some others from yanside of the mountain, over by Misery Hollow and White Lightning Creek. Silvy waved her hand in the air.

"Do we get the same kind of diplomas as the rest? And go on, if we're a mind to?"

"Of course," Miss Henderson said soothingly. "We just feel that young people who still live in the mountains have the best opportunity to collect accurate information."

Silvy examined that statement for any hint of disdain and decided that Miss Henderson meant well. She was smart, too, to have seen through Silvy's big talk yesterday.

"First come, first served on what each one of you wants to study," Miss Henderson said. "Shall I give you until after lunch to think it over?"

Silvy and Addie May and everybody else that carried their lunch were allowed to eat in the cafeteria, in case they wanted to buy anything extra, which Silvy never did.

"We can arrange for you to get free milk," one of the teachers had said last year when she had seen Silvy washing down her corn bread with a glass of free water.

"No, ma'am, thank you kindly. I get milk at home."

That was the truth, so why waste a dime on something she didn't need, even if she had a dime to spare? Let them offer their charity to somebody that could use it.

Addie May had her lunch in a brown paper bag with a spot of grease showing through. Silvy brought hers in a little covered basket that Granny had made her ownself a long while before Silvy was born.

"White oak makes the lastiest baskets you can git," Granny said. "They don't never wear out."

"What're you aimin' to pick for your subject?" Addie May asked when they were settled with their lunch at the far corner table where nobody was likely to bother them. "It don't look like a hard year, just studyin' what we know already."

Silvy didn't think it was going to be all that simple. Mostly things that looked that way didn't turn out to be so, like the time Ma went out to milk the cow and met up with a skunk.

Lud and Kel came in, Lud with a full tray of boughten food and Kel with his chipped black tin lunch bucket. Kel took out a bacon-and-cornbread sandwich and a book, which he propped up against the sugar shaker. Silvy couldn't see the title—not homework unless Kel had his own special set of books that didn't look like anybody else's.

"Look out you don't bite off your own finger by mistake," Addie May said, but Kel only glanced at her vaguely and didn't even answer.

"Where'd you get the book?" Silvy asked.

"School library," he said, not even looking up this time.

Silvy didn't remember that Kel had been all this studious last year. Mostly he was just silent—not that he could probably get a word in edgewise in the bus of an evening with Addie May and Lud sounding off and Silvy not exactly backward either.

"I thought plants," said Silvy, getting back to her topic for Appalachian Studies.

Granny could help her out with that—what the different plants were used for, maybe with an exhibit of pressed flowers and leaves to show. The more she thought about it, the better it sounded, although it was mighty old-timey and wouldn't help her jump off into tomorrow the way the magazine said. It seemed Miss Henderson's idea must be to push them all back into the coves and hollows instead of showing them a way out. Anyhow, the plant project would give Silvy plenty of time to ponder on something else, like her foolish talk about college, which gave her a headache even to think about.

"What do you mean, plants?" Lud, who believed in putting first things first, was already halfway through his second hamburger.

"For my topic," said Silvy. "Wild plants."

"I'm takin' the tame kind—corn and like that," Lud announced.

"You are?" asked Silvy.

"Yup! You get lots of stuff from corn—corn bread, them little cornhusk doll babies, brooms—"

"And corn likker," Addie May muttered in Silvy's ear.

"I heard that," said Lud, polishing off a piece of pie. "Trouble with you, Addie May, you talk too much."

"Takes one to call one," Addie May said cheerfully. "I'm going to pick weaving."

"Figured you would," said Silvy.

Addie May's mother wove so beautifully that the Guild was nigh as crazy to get her work as they were Pa's every-so-often dulcimers.

"Hey!" Lud interrupted. "You want to go to the football game Sat'dy night?"

Lud had a pretty good car, or his Pa did. It wasn't much to look at but a fast traveler, to judge from the roar it made boiling down the road sometimes in the night. Addie May'd have a good time going out with Lud, for all she talked like she thought he was so horrible.

"You!" Lud, with his mouth half full of chocolate cake, pointed his knife in Silvy's direction.

"Me? Well, I—" She couldn't, she absolutely couldn't, even if Pa would let her.

"We'll all go," said Addie May. "It's free on our activity ticket, anyway. What time you want to pick us up?"

"Never said I wanted to pick *you* up noways," said Lud, but he wasn't really mad. "Kel, you can come and keep Addie May from talkin' me to death."

Kel didn't say would he or wouldn't he. He just closed his book and stuck it back in his lunch box.

"*Me* talk *you* to death?" Addie May demanded. "Let's get out of here. Doesn't seem there's any more to eat, so you may as well quit."

They all walked out together, a solid front in case the town kids wanted to pass any remarks about mountain folks. Mostly they just looked, as though Silvy and the rest were bright green with purple trimmings. Silvy always stared back wooden-faced. She couldn't see where she looked any different from anybody else. Her hair was hanging long and straight and blonder than most, and her blue dress that she and Ma had made on the old treadle sewing machine was out of a pattern that Silvy had looked at but not bought at the dry goods store in town.

"Too short by a foot," Granny had grumbled at sight of it.

Silvy hadn't argued, but she hadn't lengthened the skirt either. Granny was part of the "then" time that Silvy was trying to get away from. At least she guessed she was trying to get away. It was funny how all the new things that she saw on TV and read about in school pulled at her while the old familiar ways she had known all her life wanted to drag her back. Right now it looked as if life were a tug-of-war and she were the rope, with no for-sure way of getting to go in either direction.

"Kel! Wait!"

Silvy hurried a little to walk along with him, not so much for his company as to get away from Lud, who was likely to bellow out something stupid where everybody could hear. Addie May wouldn't care if he did and would answer him back quick as a wink, no matter who might be listening, but Silvy didn't fancy making a spectacle of herself. Today it wasn't so hard to get away because Lud was favoring his left ankle some.

"Been fightin' a bobcat?" Addie May wanted to know.

"Licked him too!" Lud said. "Lemme tell you how it was. I was out choppin' wood for the stove—Ma's got a stitch in her back—when here come this bobcat, jumpin' down on me off the roof of the shed. Know what I done?"

"Not what you're a-goin' to tell me," said Addie May, "but tell away. I got nothin' better to do right now than listen to made-up stories."

"What I done," said Lud, undaunted, "I strangled him to death. Got his hide nailed up on the shed door curin' right now." He paused for effect. "Onliest thing I got was some scratches and turned my ankle."

"Turned your ankle runnin' away, most likely," said Addie May.

Or tripping over Pa's plow, could be. Silvy stopped in her tracks to think it over and catch her breath. Kel seemed to be in a big rush. Maybe he was running away from her, same as she was running away from Lud. Kel turned.

"You coming?" he asked. "Have to pick up a library book. No time after school."

That was another problem with having to ride the bus fifteen miles morning and afternoon. Nobody could stay after school for anything without fixing up a ride home ahead of time, and rides were scarce going to Curiosity Cove.

"What kind of book?" Silvy wanted to know.

"For Clate Fowler to look at." Kel ducked into the school library. "Have to look in the card index."

While he was looking, Silvy wandered around looking, too. She never got much chance to come in here, though last year the English teacher had given everybody time out of class to hunt references for their research papers.

"May I help you?" the librarian asked.

"Well—" Silvy had a sudden inspiration. "Would you have something on college scholarships?"

If she could get a scholarship—not the kind that people got because they were what the TV called "disadvantaged" but one that Silvy could earn herself somehow— Pa might decide it wasn't charity and let her go. The trouble was, Silvy's grades weren't the greatest. She hadn't ever actually failed anything, but until she came into town to high school from the little one-room school on Cove Creek, there had been a lot of things she'd never even heard of. There still were some, but not as many any more, thanks to TV and the radio and being around town folks some of the time. Likely it'd work the other way, too. Set some of the townies down in the middle of the mountains and they might not know a wild boar from a chipmunk.

"There's this." The librarian produced a booklet. "The government puts it out. Do you have any special college in mind?"

"No, ma'am." Until the day before yesterday she hadn't had college in her mind at all, and even yet the idea didn't have a real firm hold on her. "I'm just pondering." Dreaming was more like it, if that. "I said I would," she blurted, "so now it looks like I've kind of got to make good on it."

"Any way I can help—"

"Thank you kindly," said Silvy, shamefaced. She didn't know what had possessed her to say even as much as she had to a stranger. "I kin—can—take this home, then?"

"Better take some college catalogs, too. It's not too early to start applying."

"Yes, ma'am. I—I'd have to work the rest of the way, even if I did get a scholarship," she said painfully.

Pa, as full of pride as a porcupine was full of quills, wouldn't be pleased to hear her admitting out loud that she needed help, but the librarian was trying to give her a hand, which was hard to do without the true facts.

"Over at Highcliff, across the mountains, they have a work program. I can look up their catalog for you if you want to stop in after school."

"I go on the bus," Silvy explained, "so I couldn't."

"Tomorrow noon then." Silvy stuck the booklet into her lunch basket just as Kel came up with two books to check out, fat books that didn't look very interesting. "Well, Kelsey, what kind of luck are you having?" the librarian asked.

"Medium. I might know what I want when I see it, but seeing it's the problem."

Seeing what? Birds, flowers, clouds? Silvy couldn't imagine. It seemed Kel could actually talk if he took a notion and talk real townish, too.

He might even have talked some more, but the bell rang, and he and Silvy had to run downstairs and into class before they got marked late.

"Have you all decided what topics you want to take?" Miss Henderson asked briskly. "I'll call out your names and put down your choices."

She opened her roll book and began going down the list. Everybody seemed to have something in mind—history of the area, the building of the Blue Ridge Parkway, hunting and fishing—

32

"Plants!" said a voice.

Silvy, with her mouth opening and closing like a fish's, turned to stare at the girl who had just taken her subject —Mary Ellerbe, whose folks were root-'n'-herbers from a long way back. Wasn't it just Silvy's hard luck that Miss Henderson's roll book was done alphabetically and E came before K every single time? So now what was Silvy going to do? She gave Addie May a despairing look as the roll call got closer and closer to the K's. She'd just have to say she hadn't made up her mind yet and could she wait until tomorrow, though she couldn't see that she was going to have any more ideas tomorrow than she did today.

"Psst!"

The girl in the seat behind her slipped a wadded-up note into her hand, dangling alongside her desk. Pretending to be looking at something in her notebook, Silvy smoothed out the scrap of paper. There was just one word scrawled on it in hurried handwriting: Rocks.

"Silvy?" Miss Henderson said.

"R-rocks?" Silvy said weakly.

Somebody had saved her at the last minute, but what did Silvy care about rocks? Mountains were made of them and they made bumps in the lane and hiding places for snakes, but aside from that— They weren't even overly pretty, not like the pink and white laurel that Granny called ivy or the fields of orange tiger lilies or the lavender joe-pye weed.

"Minerals, do you mean?" Miss Henderson asked.

"I—I—" Silvy floundered helplessly.

Minerals came out of mines, so maybe the feldspar from where Pa worked once in a while would be classified as a mineral. It was the only one she knew anything about and not much at that. Kel's voice—it had never occurred to Silvy that it had a nice, pleasant sound to it—cut in.

"I had it in mind for Silverbell and me to work together

on local minerals if it suits you," he told Miss Henderson. "One person couldn't handle it alone—too much material."

Two couldn't either, if one of them was Silvy, but Kel would help her. He better had, seeing he'd gotten her into this.

"That sounds very interesting," Miss Henderson agreed. She ran through the rest of the list so everybody else could get their bids in. "I'm going to give you plenty of leeway on how you map out your work and when you do it, but I'll expect progress reports in class every week. I'll suggest background material, and we'll have field trips and guest lecturers if I can arrange it. Any questions?"

"Do we go to our other classes, same as always?" Addie May wanted to know.

"Yes, but as far as possible your work will be tailored to your Appalachian Studies. For instance, in chemistry you may want to experiment with—oh, minerals or whatever—and in history or home ec or music— I'll leave it up to you to see how they can be made to apply, and the other teachers will keep your special interests in mind."

This was going to be a funny year but interesting, too, except for not learning much about anywhere else except right here.

"Thanks." Silvy caught up to Kel as they all trooped out to the bus after school. "Except I don't know what this's all about."

"I'll show you." Kel looked off into space about two feet over Silvy's head. "We'll start first thing Saturday morning."

"Doing what?"

"Looking for rocks. Bring a lunch; we'll be going a far piece." He plunked his books down on the seat of the bus. "Here. You can look this over first."

Rock Hunters' Guide—Silvy gave it an alarmed look, but Kel didn't offer a word of comfort. He just sat down across the aisle and began reading something called *Manual of Mineralogy*. He and Silvy and Addie May were all the way home before he said another word and then only when he had managed to outstay Addie May at the foot of the lane.

"What beats me," said Silvy, "is why—"

"You're the onliest one from around here that's going to college, too," said Kel.

"*You* are?" If possible, Kel's folks were worse off for cash money than Silvy's.

"I *am!*" said Kel, with his chin stuck out a mile. "Somehow."

"Besides," said Silvy, "I don't think I am, really." She hung her head. "I—I was just sort of talking when I—"

"You don't want to go?"

The answer to that was going to take some study. From what Silvy had seen on TV, a lot of the ones that were going to college didn't think much of it, and the ones that weren't there were fussing because they couldn't get in.

"I'm not sure," she said finally.

He glowered at her as though she were an extra-low-down insect.

"If you're not sure, you won't go." He turned on his heel and headed down the road, staring at the ground as usual.

Silvy, aware of being disapproved of, noticed with interest that, like Lud, Kel was favoring one ankle a little.

"How'd you hurt your leg?" she yelled after him.

He turned and gave her a long look.

"Stranglin' bobcats," he said, unblinking.

35

"This here's partly what we're looking for." Kel had to speak up above the sound of a lot of stones slithering around in a revolving barrel at Clate Fowler's. Kel held up a hunk of rock with something green and glimmering in it. "Not that we're likely to find any. That's emerald and scarcer'n hens' teeth around here any more. Then there's sapphire and garnet and aquamarine." He picked stones out of a series of trays on a long table. "And ruby and golden beryl."

They were pretty-sounding words, every one, prettier than the real thing, rough and unpolished and tangled up with plain old rock. Just from trying to make sense out of the book Kel had loaned her, Silvy knew already that there wasn't any such thing as plain old rock, though. There were igneous rocks, sedimentary rocks, and metamorphic rocks with fancy names like pegmatite and shale and gneiss and a lot more she couldn't remember. Rocks were made up of minerals of umpteen kinds, colors, and habits. At that point, Silvy, with her brains in a whirl, had tossed the book aside and gone back by the glade to get Granny some rosemary, just right for picking, with its little bluish flowers starting to show up. Plants, now, Silvy could handle with no trouble, but rocks were what she was stuck with, ignorant as a new-laid egg.

"Best try the dump down by the old feldspar mine," said Clate, a gaunt man who didn't have much more to say than Kel, "though the summer folks likely have the stuff pretty well picked over. You'll just have to dig a little deeper." He turned irritably in his chair to ease his hurt hip. "You got a pretty day for it."

"You'll be out and going again," Kel said. "Until you are, depend on us."

For what, Silvy wondered. Hunting rocks, for one thing, it looked like, though there seemed to be plenty of them still lying around the shop in a clutter of grinding wheels, circular saws, sandpaper, sealing wax, fruit-juice cans, modeling clay, squeeze bottles, and nobody knew what else except maybe Clate. He pulled himself up to rummage on a shelf as crowded as the rest of the place.

"Keys to the truck." He tossed them to Kel.

"Ma says can you help us out eatin' a pie?" Silvy had set it down on the table on the way in and forgotten about it. "Two's most too much for us any more."

Any more—that meant with Bobby lying in the cemetery, Arvilla married and gone to live over the mountain, and only the four of them left at home.

"Glad to help you out," Clate said. "Your ma's a tasty cook."

She was, and with nothing much but homegrown stuff to do it with. If Silvy and Kel went high enough in the mountains today, they might find some late-ripening black-berries to carry home. Ma was a great one to can every-thing she could lay her hands on. Silvy's favorite—sun-preserved wild strawberries set out to thicken in sugar syrup for a few days with a mosquito net draped over the pans to keep the gnats and bees out—tasted real sum-mery in the middle of a snowstorm.

"Aquamarine I need bad," Clate said, "to set in the Gatchell girl's wedding ring."

Maybe Kel was figuring to earn college money by hunt-ing gemstones for Clate until he could get back on his own two feet again, though it'd take a mighty lot to pile up much cash that way.

"Good luck on your own looking," said Clate—whatever that meant.

Kel picked up a bulgy knapsack that he had left on the doorstep coming in and slung it on the seat of Clate's sorry old truck. Sorry as it was, it was better than walking all the way to wherever they were going. There'd be plenty of that anyway, in case Kel had it in mind to go up to the high places. While he ground away on the starter and fi-nally got the sputtering engine going, Silvy tried to remem-ber what the rocks that Kel had showed her looked like. She'd never know one of them again unless they had chunks of gems sticking out clear as day, which wasn't likely. She was going to make a spectacle of herself today, starting at rock bottom the way she was.

"Rock bottom's the word for it," she said out loud.

"H'mp?" Kel came back from some far-off place that was likely full of eighteen kinds of rock. "Clate gives me something for whatever I bring in that he can use. I put it away for book money, and you can do the same."

"Thank you kindly," said Silvy, meek as skim milk.

Without college money, she wouldn't need any book money. She had read the pamphlet the librarian had given her, but it hadn't helped a lot. Just maybe she could get a loan, but she'd have to pay it back, which she mightn't be able to do. There were scholarships for the "disadvantaged," just as she had surmised, but those she was too proud to ask for, even if Pa would let her. Almost all the rest were special, like for extra-good grades or for being the child of a World War II veteran or for somebody with the last name of Billingsford. People got funny notions about how they wanted their money spent.

"Was I a descendant of Noah Webster going to study dictionary-making, somebody'd likely give me the cash to do it," Silvy said above the clatter of the truck.

"Likely they would." Kel must have had the same thing on his mind as Silvy. "There's other ways."

"Name some." Robbing banks came to mind or making moonshine down one of the far hollows or— "Do people ever find diamonds around here?"

"No." Kel turned off the hard road onto a dirt trail that rapidly faded out to nothing much. "A few little ones up the country a long time ago." He stopped the truck with a shudder of brakes. "Diamonds aren't the onliest things that'll make you rich."

Rich! Nobody ever got rich around here out of rocks or anything else. Likely he was just talking big, though that was more Lud's style than Kel's.

"What?" asked Silvy. "What'll make you rich?"

"When I know for sure I'll tell you."

He picked up the knapsack and started off cross-country, clambering over rocks and up stony slopes. Silvy scrambled after him. Likely he was sorry already that he'd raked her in on this project. He wasn't the only one that was sorry, but if he was working on a way to get rich, Silvy wasn't aiming to be left out. She stumbled over a boulder that sprang up in her path when she wasn't looking, but Kel didn't even turn around to see if she was doing all right. He just ambled along, looking at the ground the way Silvy and Addie May had seen him doing a hundred times. At least now Silvy knew it was rocks he was looking for. There were plenty of them here, but he didn't pick up a single one to look it over.

"This's it," he said as they finally came to the bottom of a cliff chopped out of the side of the rock. "Opencut mining right here, but they worked underground, too." He gestured toward a boarded-up hole in the face of the rock. "That was the entrance to the main shaft. Whole works are abandoned now." That was all the attention he could spare for the mine itself. "Dump's over yonder."

He must mean a towering pile of leftover light-colored rock—white and gray mostly, some of it with little sparkles in it like what showed up sometimes in the dirt alongside the road or in the cleared fields.

"Mica?" she said doubtfully.

"The sparkly part is. The rest is mostly feldspar."

Kel might expect her to know what was what, but she had never been within five miles of a mine before, even an old worn-out one like this. The Kershaws were strictly mountain people, seldom out of Curiosity Cove except when Pa took a job at the feldspar plant when things got extra bad for him.

Kel opened the knapsack and took out a hammer with a pick opposite the hammerhead, plus a compass, a small magnifying glass, a horseshoe magnet, and several pieces of what looked like an old broken plate. He laid everything out on a handy flat rock.

"What do we do now?" Silvy asked.

"Look through the dump."

"OK." Silvy stared helplessly at the hill of rock, which made her feel half as big as a grain of sand. Her folks were a long-lived family—Granny's father had died at ninety-two—but Silvy doubted she'd be around long enough to work her way through all this. "When that's done, what do we do the rest of the day?"

"We could quarry a few tons of rock," said Kel, straight-faced, "only I forgot the dynamite." He turned serious again, his natural state. "That's part of a pegmatite dike. You find a heap of minerals mixed in with pegmatite."

He didn't seem to be finding a heap of anything, from the way he was picking up pieces of rock, giving them a quick look and throwing them down again. Silvy stared wistfully up to the top of the cut, rimmed with spruce pine, and on to the mountains, already blazing with reds and yellows up where the frost had already hit hard. It was a heap prettier up there than it was down here, poking through a bunch of rocks that all looked about the same: rocky.

"We git—get—all these rocks collected, and then what, besides selling them to Clate?" If Silvy was going to break her back working on a rock pile, it'd be nice to know what she was doing it for. "How's that going to tie in with our school project?"

"Depends on what we find."

That was no answer at all, but likely it was all Silvy would get, at least right away. Kel picked up a chunk of rock, looked at it critically, and dropped it into the knapsack.

"Let me see that," Silvy said, "so I'll know to save another one like it." Kel fished it out again and handed it to her. As far as she could see, it wasn't anything a person'd notice in a crowd—rough and darker colored than some. "You mean Clate can make something pretty out of that?"

"This isn't for him."

Kel laid the rock on a boulder and gave it a sharp rap with the hammer. It split open, looking not much different except for some embedded scraps of black mineral inside,

41

with a lustrous look to them like the resin that sometimes oozed out of the pine trees.

"No aquamarine there," said Silvy in disappointment.

"Nope." Kel sounded remarkably cheerful. He touched a piece of the rock with the magnet. Nothing happened. Then he rubbed one of the fragments across the broken edge of the old plate, leaving a powdery brownish streak. "Could be two or three things, maybe all of them at once."

"In that one piece? How do you find out for sure?"

"Don't, maybe, but Clate's got a book that says what to do. Different tests."

"What kind of tests?"

"Chemical, mostly."

Prying explanations out of Kel was as hard as finding gemstones in rocks. He wasn't like Lud, telling everything he knew the first fifteen minutes, with nine minutes left over when he'd told it all.

"What's the name of these minerals you think you might have a hunk of?" The only way to find out anything was to ask, according to Granny.

"Samarskite, columbite, and euxenite." He wrapped the pieces of rock in a square of old cloth this time and put them back into the knapsack. "Maybe."

"Samarskite, columbite, euxenite."

Silvy repeated the names to be sure she had them clear in her mind. The words made a jumpy little tune in her head or maybe even a poem. Samarskite had an extra-fine sound to it, like faraway places that Silvy would never in this world have a chance to see.

"Why's it called that?" she asked. "Samarskite, I mean."

"Dunno."

There must be a reason. Even Silvy's name had a reason, and minerals, being so scientific, were entitled to something more than just somebody's passing fancy. At least they weren't named Rock A, Rock B, and Rock C.

Kel was busy inspecting chunks of rocks and then tossing them aside. Silvy sat down on the ground and began looking, too—not that she was likely to know what she wanted even if she saw it.

"Here's something." Kel squinted through his little magnifying glass at another of the endless pieces of rock.

"What?" asked Silvy.

"Aquamarine crystals—little ones, but Clate doesn't need them any bigger this time."

Through the glass, Silvy could see two greenish-blue nodules stuck into the rock like the raisins Ma put in the Christmas pudding, only a lot smaller. At least aquamarine looked as though it might be pretty when Clate got it shined up—unlike samarskite, columbite, and euxenite, about which Kel had shown a heap more enthusiasm.

"You can look it up," said Kel.

"Look what up?"

"Why it's called samarskite."

"Oh, that."

She could wait on that, now that Kel had actually found some aquamarine. Silvy feverishly turned over one rock after the next, burrowing into the heap like a boomer, one of the gabbiest squirrels in the mountains, foraging for the acorns he'd buried for winter. The day was cool, but Silvy wasn't. She pushed her hair impatiently back from her face. If only she could find something, just one something! If only, in fact, she hadn't been sucked in on this rock-hunting in the first place!

Kel discovered a few more aquamarine crystals and a couple of pieces of rock that he set aside, even though they didn't have anything different about them that Silvy could see. She sat back on her heels and rested herself with another look at the forests climbing up the mountains. There she'd know her way around, but this was like some foreign country where she couldn't even speak the language. She bent again to the rock heap. Maybe if they found enough aquamarine for that wedding ring, they could quit for the day or anyway go somewhere else.

"What's that?" Silvy snatched at a piece of rock with a goldy-brown glimmer to it. Kel moved over to take a look.

"Golden beryl," he said. "Aquamarine's beryl, too, and so's emerald, if we ever get that lucky."

At least Silvy had found something and learned a couple of things, too, so the day hadn't been a total loss. Maybe the rocks didn't look so much alike after all. Why, any minute she might turn one over and find another pretty for Clate. Maybe, even, she could keep a few little pieces for herself—not the gemstones, which would be too much to expect, seeing they were worth cash money, but something that didn't amount to anything but might have if the rock had happened to shape up a little different.

"What're we going to tell Miss Henderson next week," Silvy asked, "so she'll know we've been doing something except reading out of a book?"

"We'll say we're doing preliminary research," said Kel, "to—uh—establish—" He grinned. "To establish the presence of—uh—whatever we can establish the presence of." He certainly knew a lot of high-toned words when he was of a mind to use them. "Won't know what we're going to find until we find it."

"Makes it harder when we don't know what we're looking for either," Silvy said tartly. Likely Kel knew good and well what they were looking for, and she was pretty sure it wasn't gemstones, except in passing. "Do we hunt just in old mine dumps?"

"Mostly."

His supply of words was running low again, and so was Silvy's patience. Her back ached from all the stooping and bending, and she looked yearningly at her lunch basket.

"Best take enough for two," Ma had said that morning,

packing cold biscuit, a couple of thin slices of fried ham, and a jar of sourwood honey in Silvy's basket.

"She's too young for courtin'," Pa had said from the front porch, where he was whittling a sliver of hickory to pluck a dulcimer with.

Arvilla had been almost a year younger when she quit school and got married, and Pa hadn't thought that was too young.

"This isn't courtin'," Silvy said. Kel didn't have any words to waste on courting, or time either. "You want me to fail and not get my diploma?"

Likely he didn't care much one way or another, but Silvy was his least child, who, Granny said, could "twine him around her finger like woodbine a-clamberin' up a sap-lin'." That wasn't strictly so—Pa wasn't one to be bent much one way or another once he got his mind set—but he always spoke gently to Silvy, though she didn't doubt he could talk just the opposite if he found it needful.

"Kel's a good steady boy," Ma said soothingly. "He'll make his way."

If he didn't, it wouldn't be for want of trying, Silvy thought as he worked doggedly through what looked like another ton of rock. He had a few more pieces of broken-up stuff in the knapsack, some of it with colored crystals showing in the granite and some without. Silvy had found only a few rocks that she even bothered to show to Kel, who nodded either yes or no and kept right on looking and tossing like some kind of mining machine. In Silvy's opinion, he wasn't going to be much of a teacher, being so stingy about explaining things.

"This's enough here," he said finally, standing stiffly and starting to collect all the things he had laid out on the flat rock.

"You're not quitting?" said Silvy. "We could easy finish up by Christmas."

He didn't change expression.

"We'll come back next week. Pickin's are slim today." Did he expect some more rocks to hatch out in a week like Ma's banty chicks out of a setting of eggs? "I heard there was a rock slide up by the bald. We'll try there."

"And eat there, too," Silvy said firmly. He acted like the type that would rather hunt rocks than eat, but Silvy wasn't all that crazy yet. "We have to keep our stren'th up."

She knew she was being contrarious, but she was tired and dirty and about to starve.

"You bein' so little and wispy, people'll walk right over you," Ma had said once, "unless you git a little spunk and speak up for yourself."

It wasn't spunk Silvy lacked, not when she was with mountain folks. Other times, she tended to keep her mouth shut and her ears open, so's to learn something if she was lucky. Maybe Kel had the same idea, though he carried it a little far. Kel finally stopped the puffing truck up a wavering side road that twisted deeper into the mountains.

"Road's about give out anyway," he said.

"Food!" Silvy wailed.

"Soon's we get up there," said Kel, sympathetic as a chunk of granite. "It's a real pretty place."

They scrambled through a jungle of rhododendron growing head-high and came out finally into an open space full of goldenrod and purple asters.

"Blackberries!" said Silvy. "Over by the trees. They'll go fine with our lunch, and then we'll pick some for our folks."

"Could," said Kel, already poking with his prospector's pick at a boulder that looked as though it had slid down from up the slope with a bunch of other rocks.

"Blackberries'll taste better'n rocks next winter," Silvy said.

Kel might not think so, but his ma would. Kel's folks

just barely scratched out a living on their place, even though his pa had a sometime job on the county roads in the summer.

Kel, likely pondering on rocks, hadn't put much in his lunch bucket, so he took kindly to the ham and biscuit Ma had sent. Between that and the sourwood honey, they had a good meal, though Silvy's mouth was watering for a taste of those blackberries.

"I'll pick, and you hunt rocks," she said. "Blackberries I know for sure when I see 'em, but I could pass over a likely piece of rock and never know any different."

Silvy tossed out the leftover biscuit crumbs for the striped chipmunks, who darted back and forth watching her with their beady eyes. It was nice up here with the spruce pines, the rhododendron bushes, the blue mountains rolling away for miles and miles, and the air with a nice fresh smell to it. None of this had a thing in the world to do with the "relevant" things that TV was always carrying on about—wars and air pollution and poverty and riots and bombs and drugs. Still and all, popping blackberries into Kel's empty lunch bucket and sometimes into her own mouth, Silvy couldn't feel guilty about not getting worked up just yet over all the outside problems. What could she do anyway until she got her own head above water? Besides, she'd about winded herself getting up here, so she figured she'd earned the right to enjoy it.

"Best if you quit now." Silvy came close to choking on a blackberry as Kel appeared at her elbow. "Bear's pickin' berries on the far side of the patch." Sure enough, squinting through the bushes, Silvy could make out a dark bulk. Kel swept up Silvy's lunch basket as they crept back across the bald. "We can duck around thisaway and keep downwind. Besides, there's some slid-down rock yonder I might look at goin' by."

"You can risk your life for a few hunks of rock if you're

of a mind to," Silvy sputtered, "but I'm aimin' to save mine and keep right on a-goin'."

She didn't think any bear that'd leave a patch of ripe blackberries purely for the fun of chasing people was overly smart, but maybe bears were like folks, not all real reasonable. Kel stopped long enough to pry loose a chunk of rock embedded with flat greenish-yellow formations.

"H'm. We might could—"

"I wouldn't come no farther thisaway, friends." A voice, hoarse as a bullfrog's, spoke from a tangle of trees and shrubbery. "You kin git down to your truck a-follerin' along to the right."

Silvy peered in the direction of the voice but could see absolutely nothing except the crown of a black felt hat and a flash of sunlight against something metallic—a rifle or Silvy had never seen one.

"Obliged for the directions. We could easy a-got lost." Kel's voice was carefully relaxed as he gestured Silvy to head to the right through the rhododendron thicket. "I'm a curious feller, though. Is that your own personal bear that's a-standin' behind you?"

There was a terrified yell, followed by a writhing of the bushes, as though a high wind had hit them, and a crashing sound as something or somebody made a fast retreat.

"Run!" Kel grabbed Silvy's hand and rushed her down the slope at breakneck speed. They slid the last few feet to the truck and piled in helter-skelter with blackberries, lunch basket, knapsack, rocks, and prospector's hammer. Kel ground on the starter, which caught after a breathtaking moment, and they careened down the rocky road.

"That bear!" Silvy gasped. "Shouldn't we go see if—"

"Wasn't any bear," said Kel, "except the one picking blackberries. Just a notion of mine to draw off the man's attention till we got gone."

Silvy shivered.

"Do you think he'd 've taken a shot at us?"

"Wasn't figurin' on it or he wouldn't 've warned us, but folks that nervous can get real notiony." He glanced down at Silvy, who had her head stuck under the dashboard. "You can sit up. No call to be scared now."

"I'm not scared," said Silvy. "I'm picking up our black-berries that got spilt." That about being scared was purely talk, but she wanted to laugh, too. "I'd give a nickel to 've seen his face when you called out about the bear."

"Likely it shook him some." Kel frowned. "He couldn't be real smart or he'd never have fallen for it. You figure I lost that last piece of rock?"

Silvy chased a blackberry around the floor of the cab and came up for air.

"They're not mashed too bad." Blackberry cobbler would be tasty for supper if Silvy got home in time for Ma or Granny to fix it. "That rock with the greeny-yallery in it?" She rooted around on the seat. "Here it is. What's so great about it?"

Kel beat an angry tattoo on the wheel with his fist.

"I don't know!" he said furiously. "All I got is maybes." His voice sank almost to a whisper. "I'm so dern ignorant, I just about make myself sick some days."

"Why, Kelsey McLeod!" Silvy knew how it felt not to know things. Why, until a couple of days ago she hadn't known that one rock was much different from any other. "You're the smartest boy I know!"

That wasn't saying a whole lot, with only Lud and a few others to compare with, but Silvy didn't doubt that Kel knew more than most, even if he was so closemouthed about telling it. He got closemouthed again right away, mumbling something that Silvy couldn't catch. More than likely he was ashamed that he'd admitted out loud that he wasn't entirely satisfied with himself, especially to a girl.

He didn't say a single word until he stopped at the foot of her lane.

"Here's half the berries for your ma," said Silvy, dividing them up fair and square.

"Thanks," he said, almost inaudibly.

"See you." Silvy's voice was uncertain.

He nodded and drove away to return Clate's truck. Silvy would have liked to go, too, to hear what Clate had to say about the rocks they'd brought back, but she hadn't wanted to ask. Kel wasn't the only one that had his pride. She almost let go of hers long enough to call after him to see if he was going to the football game with her and Lud and Addie May tonight, but he wouldn't have been able to hear her anyway above the rattle of Clate's truck. Likely he'd have forgotten all about the game by now, and he never had said he'd go in the first place.

Not only that, on account of his being so wrought up about how ignorant he thought he was, she hadn't even asked him why he thought the man with the rifle had run them off and scared them about out of their wits—Silvy's wits anyway, though Kel had been making tracks, too, like the devil was after him.

"Oh, it's you!" Granny peered out of the shop. "I'm purely glad it warn't some more of them fotched-on furriners. Been pesterin' me half the day with their foolish talk and wantin' to take my picture. A body'd think they'd never seen a granny-woman before."

Maybe they never had seen one like Granny, with her sunbonnet and her long dress made by the same pattern she'd used all her life. Silvy was used to it, but it might look like a movie costume to people from away.

"Did they buy anything?" That was the important thing right now.

"Cornhusk dolls, a few of the little ones, they bein' the cheapest things we got, but two of your pa's chairs went.

Woman said they was quaint." Her face brightened. "You goin' to stay down here now?"

Silvy'd rather go up to the house and get cleaned up some, but Granny never liked to tend the shop. Silvy didn't so much either, but she could do it and leave Ma and Granny free to work on things to sell. Besides, it gave Silvy a chance to take a look at the outlanders that stopped by and see how they were different from her own self. She could do that on TV, too, but folks talking natural about everyday things would give her a better idea of how life really was out yonder.

"Your young man didn't stay long." Granny gave Silvy a sharp look.

"He had to take Clate's truck back."

"No hurry, I'd a-thought. Clate cain't drive it noways. When I was young, the boys didn't go running off from pretty girls like were skeered of their shadows."

Pretty girls! Kel might have noticed if Silvy was a pretty rock, though even then he seemed to be a heap more interested in the ones that didn't look like much. Silvy headed the talk in another direction.

"We got Clate some aquamarine for Sue Gatchell's wedding ring."

"Who's she a-marryin'? Last I heard she had her eye on— You know the one, red hair like a fox, over by—" She gave an impatient toss of her head. "I'll have to go ask your ma. I got a memory I'd let go for a bargain or trade in on a new one."

She started on up the lane, mumbling irritably to herself. Silvy ran after her with the blackberries.

"One of your cobblers'd go nice if you're not too wore out."

"Wore out! What'd I be wore out with? Ain't done an honest lick of work all day except make another Silvy doll to take the place of the one I sold."

"Who bought it?" Silvy asked.

"Now, then, that'd be a-tellin'," Granny cackled. " 'Twasn't for the one that paid for it, that I'll say."

"Somebody from around here?"

"Between here and the state of Virginny." Granny did love to tantalize. "Well, if you want cobbler, I'll have to be a-movin'."

Silvy sat herself down on one of the chairs that hadn't been sold yet. There were only three left, though she thought Pa might have a couple more finished out in the shop and waiting for the legs to age good and grab ahold of the rungs. She just hoped it wasn't Lud that had bought that doll. She couldn't imagine who else, though. She wasn't acquainted with all that many boys, and the doll must have been bought by a boy or Granny wouldn't have plagued Silvy about it. It would be just like Lud to dangle the doll on the windshield of his car to pester her. No use fretting, though. The cornhusk dolls were for sale, the same as chairs and quilts and dulcimers and sourwood honey, and anybody had a right to buy.

Things were getting real mysterious around here, what with whoever it was that had fallen over Pa's plow and the man that had driven Silvy and Kel off the bald and the doll buyer that Granny was making so much to-do about. Whether any of them were tied up with the rest, Silvy didn't have the first idea. Besides, she'd better spend her thinking time learning about rocks, so she wouldn't be entirely a dead weight.

A woman drove up and admired Ma's newest quilt—Rainbow's End, a pattern that Ma had made up out of her head—and said how much was it and she'd be back.

"Thank you. Glad to show you," said Silvy. "And we won't spend the money yet either," she added under her breath.

The evening shadows were creeping across the mountains when she locked the shop up and trudged up the lane to the house. She just about cracked her jaw yawning. Chasing after rocks all day wasn't extra restful. It'd be purely a pleasure to go straight to bed the minute she finished her share of the cobbler, which was sending a rich juicy smell all through the kitchen.

"I nigh forgot," said Granny. "Addie May stopped by and said be ready at seven. She and Lud'll pick you up down by the road."

Silvy sighed. In town, boys'd come right to the door, but it wasn't sensible here to shake a car off its foundations rumbling up the rocky lane. She'd be glad to get to the game any old how to see how the town looked all lit up at nighttime, but she'd just as soon Lud wasn't in the crowd. Of course if he wasn't, none of them would be going because Lud was the one that had the car, so she shouldn't be looking gift horses in the mouth.

She headed down the lane a little before seven. It was darker than the inside of a boot until she got her night sight, and then she could see the stars shining bright up yonder, though the moon hadn't risen yet. She froze as a dark figure loomed up alongside.

"Don't be scared." Kel's quiet voice came to her. "It's me."

Silvy breathed again.

"Thought it was a bear. Truth to tell, I'm about beared out just lately. What did Clate say?"

"The aquamarine's just what he had in mind. He's studyin' now should he try to facet 'em or cut 'em cabochon." He read Silvy's silence like a book. "Cabochon means polished smooth all over. Faceted means sparkly. He's wantin' some more golden beryl, too, if we can find some." He hesitated. "He'll keep track of what we bring in and pay us every month according to what he can use. Half to you, half to me."

That didn't seem quite fair, seeing it was Kel who knew

the different minerals when he saw them. On the other hand, traipsing around in rock piles was harder on Silvy's constitution than it was on Kel's.

"How about samarskite, columbite, and euxenite?" she asked. "Were they, or not?"

"I'll have to take 'em in to the chemistry lab to find out for sure."

He was almost gabby, but he clammed up again when Addie May crossed the road to meet them. Lud drove up, bathing them all in the glare of his headlights. Addie May exchanged glances with Silvy and hopped into the front seat beside Lud.

"Looky here," he said, "who said you could—"

"I said so," Addie May retorted blithely. "I want to hear some more about that bobcat you strangled. 'Tisn't every day you get to talk to somebody that's strangled a bobcat."

"We saw a—" Something on the back ledge brushed against Silvy's neck. "Good grief, what's that?"

If it was that cornhusk doll made to look like Silvy, she'd toss it out the window first chance she got, she surely would! She turned to look into the glowing red eyes of a toy dog that nodded its head up and down with the motion of the car.

"That there's a bloodhound," said Lud.

"Or one of those bobcats that got away," said Silvy. "Kel and I saw a bear today while we were out hunting rocks, and a—"

Kel put a warning hand on her arm.

"What'd you do?" Addie May asked.

"Kel pushed him off the mountain. Last we saw, he was bouncing down the side of Old Baldy. Folks below must've thought it was an avalanche."

"First off, though, I looked at his teeth to see how old he was," Kel put in. "I made it twenty-seven years and three months even."

Lud speeded up.

"I got to drop some things off at my Cousin Henry's," he said. "Hey, is that car a-follerin' us?"

"Must be," said Addie May. "If it isn't ahead, it's bound to be following."

"We'll get rid of him," Lud said uneasily. "I don't like folks tail-gatin' me thataway."

He stomped down on the accelerator, and they plunged dizzily around the curves, with the lights spraying ahead to turn the eyes of a rabbit crouched beside the road into a pair of gemstones. Silvy clutched Kel's arm as the car veered around an especially sharp curve. Who'd ever have thought that this old car could go so fast and so smooth, too? Must be a lot heftier engine inside than a person would think from the outside.

"You lost him," said Addie May. "You can slow down now. I'm not aiming to get kilt going to a football game."

Lud didn't slow down much, though, until he got into town. He veered down a side street, stopped in front of a little house, and lumbered in with a carton that he took out of the trunk. He looked like a bear his own self, big and clumsy and shambling. He hadn't any more than gotten back before a black car with two men in it cruised slowly by. Lud lifted a hand in greeting.

"Nice night for ridin'," he called out, polite, for once, but not as though he much meant it.

"Who's that?" Addie May asked as the men drove on past.

"Car that was follerin' us back yonder," Lud said in an innocent-type voice. "What you figure they'd be wantin'?"

"I can think of a few things," Addie May said darkly. "If you've gone and dragged us into anything along with yourself, I'll— Well, are we going to the game or aren't we?"

It was real pretty downtown, with the neon lights all

going and people walking up and down looking in the store windows. It was prettier yet out at the football field, full of more lights and color and band music.

"Here're some good seats." Addie May steered them into places halfway up, where they could see everything.

The view of the opposite bleachers put Silvy in mind of the mountains right now, with all the reds and yellows and browns showing up like patchwork and the green from the spruce pine to set the whole thing off.

"We saw you today up by the bald." Mary Ellerbe leaned over from the next row back to talk into Silvy's ear. "We was huntin' 'sang."

Silvy wished she had been hunting ginseng, too, or anything else that grew, instead of clambering all over after a lot of rocks.

"Any luck?"

It was politeness to ask but not about exactly where—probably hidden way back someplace. People were close-mouthed about where they found things. Ginseng was a favorite with the root-'n'-herbers, who got a good price for it at the botanical place in town. The plant was easy to spot this time of year, with the bright red fruit and the leaves turning yellow. Granny said it wasn't good for a thing in the world except in folks's minds, but the people off in China set a heap of store by it.

"Got some," said Mary. "Not much. You left real quick. That bear scare you?"

"Him and—" Silvy stopped, remembering that, for some reason, Kel didn't want her to talk about the man with the rifle. "Why didn't you give a holler?"

"We were over a piece and couldn't get to you anyways. Wouldn't even a-known it was you except your hair showed up so good." She tossed her head. "Lucky thing for me I got my bid in on the herbs afore you. I wouldn't hardly a-known what else to take."

"Rocks're real fascinating." Silvy wasn't about to give Mary Ellerbe the satisfaction of thinking she had put Silvy out any. "I know all about plants already."

That was maybe a little extreme, but compared to rocks, she did know a lot about plants—not to brag on herself over much. She might not know as much as the Ellerbes because the whole tribe, from their granny down to the least little shirttail boy, combed the mountains for golden-seal and bloodroot and wild cherry bark and a dozen others to make their tax money—eating money, too, in bad years. Silvy wouldn't mind doing it her own self but the Ellerbes knew all the best places and got there first every time, though Granny knew a few spots on their own place that kept her supplied with what she needed for coughs and the collywobbles and croup back when Silvy was a lap baby.

"We found some real pretty aquamarine." Silvy couldn't keep from bragging a little. "And some golden beryl. Clate Fowler's going to make some pretties out of 'em."

"It's gems you're after, then?"

"Partly," Silvy said loftily. "No way to know for sure what we'll find until we find it."

She was about to add something about getting rich, too —which she'd have regretted the minute the words were out of her mouth—but just then a big yell went up, and she turned around to watch the football team trot out onto the field.

She had looked at football some on TV, but this was the first time she had ever seen it for real because nobody had ever offered to fetch her into town for it before. Pa wouldn't have let her come tonight either if Addie May and Kel hadn't been along, too. The game looked mighty different out in the fresh crisp air with the bright lights shining down and everybody whooping and hollering and the cheerleaders turning handsprings. Addie May had maneuvered around so Silvy was between her and Kel, with Lud scowling on the far side of Addie May. That way Silvy didn't have to listen to him loudmouthing all over the place. She was grateful he'd carried them to the game, and she'd say so when he got them safe home, but for now she was going to wipe him out of her mind.

She gave a little wriggle of pleasure. She felt as though she was in a whole new world, a million miles away from Curiosity Cove. The funny thing was, she didn't feel all nervous and keyed up, wondering was she doing things right. She was just sitting here, same as everybody else that had been going to football games all their lives. She must look all right because there wasn't a soul giving her so much as a glance except maybe Kel, who wasn't looking at her so much as through her and out the other side, thinking about rocks, more than likely.

She stared down at the field, where there was a lot of scrambling and running going on. She didn't rightly understand most of it, but seeing nobody could read her mind, it didn't much matter. When everybody else stood up and yelled, she did, too, biggest copycat ever was born. Maybe getting out of the mountains and into the town— not this town especially, but just any old one— wouldn't be as scary as she'd figured. She'd have to be careful what she said and how she said it, but it wouldn't be hard to keep her mouth shut most of the time. She was so busy imagining herself walking around somewhere far off and then going to a party or a play that half the game was over and the band marching up and down the field in fancy patterns before she got back to where she actually was.

"Lud, you goin' to buy us a bite to eat?" Addie May sniffed hungrily at a wrapped-up hot dog that was being passed from hand to hand to somebody farther down the row. "I'm about to starve to death."

"Kel kin save your life." Lud stood up and worked his way over half a dozen pairs of feet. "I got to meet some guys."

"Meet away," said Addie May. "Just get back in time to carry us home."

"What'll it be, Addie May?" Kel jingled what didn't sound like very many coins in his pocket. "And Silvy?"

"I don't want anything," Addie May said quickly. "I just thought maybe you folks did." She stood up, too. "Let's us walk around some—get the kinks out of our legs."

A crowd was milling around back of the bleachers, where the Pep Club was selling soft drinks and popcorn. Out in the parking lot Silvy spotted Lud's car, with a bunch of boys, Lud in the middle of them, leaning on the fenders, smoking cigarettes and drinking colas out of paper cups. Lud was talking fourteen to the dozen.

"Strangling that bobcat for the seventeenth time," Addie May said.

Silvy just hoped it wasn't anything worse than that. If Lud's relation did make blockade, he might be peddling some of it tonight, though it didn't seem he'd be all that dim-witted right out here practically in the open. What other people did wasn't any business of hers anyway, except that she'd like to get home in one piece. She gave Addie May a worried glance, but Addie May wasn't fretting any, from the looks of her.

"Cola?" Kel, stuck with two girls, likely figured he had to do something, and colas were about the best he could offer, if that.

"Well, I—" Silvy began to refuse, but then she figured that'd hurt his pride worse than his pocketbook. "Why, that'd be nice."

Silvy and Addie May hung around the edge of the mob pushing up to the soft drink stand and let Kel fight his way to the counter. Silvy listened to the voices around her.

"If he hadn't lost his blockers, we'd have had a touchdown sure."

"Just a few kids, I thought, but a lot more crashed. My folks absolutely flipped."

"Why not?" A girl's smooth voice, mixed in with music from a transistor radio, came from back of Silvy somewhere. "They go to this school, too."

It was a genuine town voice, like most of the others. Silvy could imitate it fairly well, as she did every school day as soon as she set foot in the town. Kel did the same, Silvy had noticed, but Addie May and Lud didn't bother, not expecting to live anywhere else but in the hills. Silvy didn't exactly expect to either, but at least she was having to give the matter some thought on account of having talked so big in class that time.

"She's about the best," the voice went on, and Silvy turned to look.

It was Jan Colby, in a sweater and plaid skirt, talking to another girl and a couple of boys. Silvy was wearing a sweater, too, hand-made by Granny, and a matching blue wool skirt, courtesy of Pa's sheep and some blue dye made from the indigo plants Granny fussed around with in a little patch back by the vegetable garden. Altogether, Silvy looked as good as Jan and maybe a little bit better. It didn't have to be clothes that made the difference between town and country, but the difference was there, plain as day. Life style was what they called it on TV, but mostly, except for a documentary once in a while, it was town and city life that the programs bore down on, with their dishwashers and freezers and clothes dryers that didn't depend on sunshine and a brisk breeze to make them work.

Kel came back with three paper cups of cola, carrying them real careful so they didn't slosh over.

"Thank you," said Silvy. "I was thirstier than I thought."

A hand touched her arm.

"Sylvia?" It was Jan Colby, to the tune of "Purple and Blue" from the little radio in her hand. "Could you speak to me a minute?"

"Her name's Silvy," Addie May put in. "Short for Silverbell."

"Sorry about that." Jan flushed up a little bit—not used to getting things wrong, probably. "You're in Miss Henderson's special class, aren't you?"

"Yes." Silvy almost said "ma'am" but stopped herself just in time. She was as good as Jan any old day. "Kelsey's in there, too, and Addie May and—" There wasn't any point in mentioning Lud until she found out what Jan wanted.

"I'm chairman of student programs for assembly this year," said Jan, smooth as cream again, "and I want you to be on my committee—one person from every home room."

"Well, I—" Silvy rummaged around in her mind for a good excuse or even a bad one. In a way, she wouldn't mind doing it—it'd be a way of learning something new—but in another, she was scared. What good would she be on a program committee or any other kind of committee? "I—I just don't—"

Everybody turned to stare as a big burst of male laughter came from over by Lud's car. Lud headed up toward the stadium, talking in a voice mighty near loud enough to be heard clear back in Curiosity Cove.

"Biggest bobcat ever I seen!" he roared.

Silvy gave up on her excuses.

"All right," she murmured to Jan, and began edging her way nervously toward the bleachers before Lud could spot her and the rest in the thinning crowd. "I'll do it."

"Come out, come out, wherever you are!"

Silvy spoke sternly to the innards of a piece of rock that looked like nothing special, but minerals, especially the kind Kel fancied, were sneaky. Samarskite, which he had found hardly any of, was likely to be embedded in something else and wasn't guaranteed to show up shiny black, the way the book said, except on a fresh break. Columbite was mighty nigh as retiring. Autunite, though, the greeny-yallery mineral that Kel had found up by the bald along with the bear and the man with the rifle, was pretty enough, in a modest way.

"Autunite forms in seams in pegmatites," Kel read out of a beat-up field guide that Clate had loaned him. "Result of the alteration of uraninite."

"Oh, me!" More words that didn't mean much to Silvy, though maybe uraninite had something to do with uranium, which was tangled up with atom bombs.

"I don't guess we'll be going up there any more," Silvy said.

The bald was a sightly spot, with or without blackberries, bears, and men with guns, but Kel had picked a good place today, too, up the slope from his pa's place, where Mr. McLeod had blasted out the side of the hill to get a root cellar.

"Later, maybe." Kel whacked at a chunk of rock with a prospector's hammer.

"You think it was a blockader, and us about to stumble over his still?" Silvy said.

September and October were supposed to be good months for making moonshine—not too warm, not too cool, and lots of leaves still on the trees for cover.

"Could be." That was a safe answer that didn't get Kel very far out on a limb.

"The air smelled kind of yeasty." That might be mostly imagination. Think something over long enough, and you could add all kinds of frills and fancies without really meaning to. "Or maybe it was the blackberries."

"Or bear. Get to leeward of them, and they're real aromatic."

Kel didn't show the first sign of caring whether the man with the rifle had been a blockader or somebody getting himself some deer meat where he shouldn't. Mostly mountain folks didn't inquire into things that didn't concern them, but there was no law against wondering. Besides, Silvy didn't take to having a rifle pointed at her—unneighborly, at the least, and downright dangerous besides.

"He doesn't own the mountain," she grumbled.

People around here roamed where they pleased, hunting

bear, gathering galax leaves, picking berries. Who cared, with forests and mountains as far as the eye could see?

"Here's something red." Silvy handed over a piece of rock with a rosy glimmer to it. "I looked up about that samarskite. It's called after a Russian engineer, Colonel M. Samarski, and columbite is named for Columbia, which is what they used to call the U.S.A." She triumphantly produced her final piece of information. "And euxenite is from a Greek word that means hospitable, because it has a bunch of other minerals in with it, like inviting all the relations to dinner."

"Dictionary's a handy thing," Kel said dryly.

Silvy gave him a suspicious look.

"You knew all the time!" And her swallowing her lunch fast every day so she'd have time to look things up in the school library!

"Not that, I didn't," Kel said.

Silvy waited expectantly, though she should have known better. Kel wasn't about to say what he did know, which was probably plenty, in spite of all his talk about being so ignorant.

"How're you going to be a teacher if—"

She was acting real crosswise, but it was aggravating to spend every Saturday chasing rocks without getting overmuch information from Kel except for his holding out a hunk of rock and saying, "This here's like what we're looking for."

"I'm not figuring to be a teacher," he said.

A good thing, too, in Silvy's opinion. She clamped her mouth tight shut. He could wait all day before she'd open it again to ask what he did have in mind to be. He waited for a good five minutes while Silvy concentrated on rocks before he finally said, "Mineralogist."

So now she could go and look that up, too, to see how a mineralogist earned a living. Hunting for minerals the way they were doing wasn't going to make anybody rich very soon—or ever, as far as Silvy could see.

"But if I *was* going to be a teacher," he went on, "I wouldn't do it by telling people everything. I'd make them dig it out for themselves mostly, same as I have to."

He handed back the rock she had just showed him.

"You got yourself some garnet there," he said. "Pass me back the book. Might be some real good stuff mixed in here."

What did he want, Silvy wondered, that'd be better than garnet, which Clate could work up into pretty jewelry? She kept forgetting that beauty and brilliance didn't seem to be what Kel had in mind.

"We'll keep on here a while," he decided. "We're looking for something dark-colored."

"Blackish, brownish, or grayish," Silvy said resignedly.

That included most of the mountainside that wasn't covered with trees and bushes and maybe some of that, too, but Silvy didn't care where she looked. Wherever it was, she ought to be home helping Ma pick Concord grapes for jelly to put out on the stand and to store for their own winter eating. They'd best sell everything they could right away, because this month would bring the last big rush of visitors up to look at the color on the mountains. After that it would be slim picking until spring brought them all back again.

Silvy straightened up and rested her eyes on the bright tapestry of trees that covered the slopes. Pretty soon there'd be nothing left except the dark green of spruce and fir, with snow for trimming. She supposed Kel would drag her out to hunt rocks in the wintertime, too. In a way it would be nice to be so fired up about something, even rocks, but Silvy wasn't. The gemstones were pretty, though not as pretty as flowers and trees, but the others, with their tongue-twisting names, left her no better than lukewarm. What did they have to do with—well, with anything that Silvy was fretting about? Unless she and Kel hit an unexpected diamond mine, all the rocks in the world weren't going to get Silvy out of here and into the bright world outside. She couldn't even get to Jan Colby's committee meetings because, as usual, she couldn't stay after school unless she wanted to walk fifteen miles home.

"But you must know somebody you could get a ride with once in a while," Jan had protested above the sound of the transistor, tuned in on "Weeping Willow." "Some of the neighbors going home from work?"

"Nobody out our way works in town," Silvy had said.

Pa had, of course, or anyway halfway between, but he'd had to thumb his way a good share of the time because the car didn't want to start of a morning without a push down the lane and sometimes not then.

"You can stay in town with me some night," Jan had said, likely sorry for Silvy because she didn't have any way to get around.

That would be the day, Silvy staying at the sprawling Colby house with its wide lawn that the bus passed on the way to school every morning. Jan's father was the head man at the bank, sitting dressed up all day long in a big office with a rug that looked two inches thick and a little sign on his desk that said Douglas Colby, President. Silvy had seen him just one time out of the corner of her eye when she went in to start a savings account with five dollars she got last year for tending the feldspar company's doctor's baby the day of his mother-in-law's funeral.

Silvy didn't much like to earn money from other people's sorrows, but Doc's wife had sent word she couldn't get her usual sitter and would take it as a favor if Silvy would help her out. The money was still in the bank, maybe up to $5.27 by now, which showed how you could get rich in a hundred years if you put your money out to interest. By rights Silvy should have turned it over to Pa in the first place, but he'd more than likely have made her give it back, which she couldn't do without hurting Doc's feelings. He felt beholden to everybody around Curiosity Cove because the menfolks took him bear-hunting sometimes.

Silvy sighed. Figuring out the right way to do was real complicated, especially when a person got mixed up with the folks in town, which was out of Silvy's territory. They weren't the only ones that had to be handled like eggs, though. Look at Lud, all bluster and blow, and— Silvy shot a sideways look at Kel. He was a deep one, too, with things going on in his head that Silvy didn't even pretend to guess at.

"We want to get us a big batch of rocks every time we come out now." Kel wrapped one up carefully in a piece of newspaper and put it into the knapsack. "Then when the weather's bad, we can run tests on the ones we can't identify just by looking."

So much for the breathing space that Silvy had looked forward to but wasn't going to get.

From reading the field guide, she knew some of the ways to tell what was which just by looking: color, shine, hardness, the shape of the crystals. There were a whole lot more tests, including some that Kel worked on in the chemistry lab. He and Clate were rigging up some equipment in Clate's shop, too, so rain or shine, nobody would get to rest on Saturdays.

"Almost forgot." Kel reached into his pocket and hauled out four tired-looking dollar bills. "We earned us eight dollars off of Clate, and this's your half."

"Well, thanks."

Silvy tucked the money into the pocket of the faded old blue jeans that Granny thought looked so sorry. She hadn't rightly earned anything like four dollars, unless Kel was counting all the time she had looked for things she didn't find. What she'd do, she'd put it in the bank along with her $5.27. Ma already had the tax money hidden away on the top shelf of the cupboard in an old teapot with the spout broken off, so she didn't actually need Silvy's money right now. Silvy quieted her conscience by telling herself that she could draw the money out for Ma if need be. In the meantime, she could fool herself by calling it her Getaway Fund. She scowled. A far piece she'd get with $9.27. She stood up and dusted off her hands.

"I better go," she said. "I promised Granny to spell her at the roadside so she can help Ma with the grape jelly."

Besides, they wanted to finish the last little bit on a new quilt to have it ready for anybody that might be wanting to buy. On pretty days they sometimes set up the quilting frame alongside the shop because it seemed to fascinate the travelers. Most of them wouldn't buy a quilt, but they would something else, to pay for watching the quilting.

Quilts! Like just about everything else in Silvy's life, they were what the TV programs called "irrelevant to present-day living." Folks had to keep warm, same as they always had, but even if they did have quilts, they were mostly made out of cloth printed all over instead of little pieces of goods sewed together to make a pattern, like Bear Track or Rainbow's End or Thunder and Lightning. Just the same, nobody made prettier quilts than Ma and Granny, though it took hours of patient piecing and figuring, besides all the fine little quilting stitches done in their own special pattern.

Kel got up, too, but not as though he much wanted to. He might not have anything to do at home—he had three younger brothers who helped around the place—but Silvy just had to have a little time off.

"Don't quit on account of me," she said.

She knew the way home, just down the slope a quarter

of a mile and across the road, but Kel picked up his knapsack, field guide, and all his rock-hunting equipment and tagged along.

"I have to ask Clate something anyway," he said.

If it wasn't for the grape jelly, Silvy would have gone with him, not because she understood much that was going on at Clate's, with saws slicing up rocks and polishers buffing them and drums rolling around to shine them up extra fine, but because if she looked at genuine specimens long enough, she might be able to recognize them when she met them somewhere else.

"I'd like the loan of the field guide," she said, "if you won't be needing it the rest of the day."

The guide had some pictures and a lot of facts about the color of rocks, where they were mostly found and what they were used for. What Silvy liked best, next to the pictures in color, were the drawings showing the shapes of the crystals, which didn't usually come out very sharp in the specimens except under the magnifying glass.

Silvy headed down an overgrown path that Kel must have worn long ago coming up here to hunt for rocks.

"Look yonder!" she said. "Hearts-bustin'-with-love." Kel stared at her with an alarmed expression, like maybe she'd lost her wits. "That bush. Folks 've got a lot of other names for it—wahoo, spindlebush, jewel-box, euonymus—but this'n's the best." Kel walked over to take a good look at red-lined seed pods bursting open to show the scarlet seeds inside. "Didn't you ever take notice before?"

It'd be easy enough to skip over a lot of shrubs that were green and nothing else, but this one practically stood up and yelled, "Look at me!" Once Ma had made a quilt by the same name in scarlet, green, and white, the prettiest she'd ever sewed except maybe Rainbow's End.

"There's a song about it, too," Silvy said.

Pa could sing it if the notion happened to strike him,

which it didn't except about once in a month of Sundays. Kel gave her a thoughtful look.

"You know a lot about plants and such."

Of course she did. Why else would she have picked them for her subject if she could have had her druthers instead of that Mary Ellerbe?

"Just because I'm purely ignorant about rocks," Silvy said tartly, "it's no sign I'm a know-nothing about everything else in the wide world. Give me the loan of your knife a minute. I might cut a bouquet to pretty up the shop."

And to sell, too, if anybody came along to buy.

"Hearts-bustin'-with-love, huh?" Kel said, solemn as a hoot owl. "Fits real well."

Silvy couldn't imagine Kel's heart bustin' with love except for a rock, but she couldn't fault him for that. For one thing, it took money to take the girls out, and Kel would be needing every cent of his for college. Even so, she couldn't see right now how he was going to get there, any more than she could her own self.

She cut a big batch of the shrub. Besides making bouquets, she could maybe package some of the seeds to sell. Pretty soon she and Ma would cut bittersweet where it crept along the rail fences and hang it up in bunches across the front of the roadside cabin to coax people to stop.

"What's that over there, then?" Kel asked as they pushed their way through a tangle of bushes that had grown over the path.

Silvy looked all around. He wouldn't be asking her about a rock, so he must mean something else, though there wasn't anything remarkable in sight except a big old sourwood with its leaves red as fire. She gestured.

"You mean that yonder? That sourwood?"

He nodded. Silvy didn't know where he had been looking all his life, not to notice sourwood. Take it back; she did too know. He'd been looking at rocks.

"It has white flowers like bells in the spring," Silvy said, "curving down real pretty. The bees like it fine, too—sweet eating and sweet looking off the same tree."

That way of putting it might be a little too fancified for Kel, but it wouldn't hurt to let him know there was something interesting on earth besides rocks. On any other subject, he wasn't a whole lot better than one of Granny's fotched-on furriners. For just a minute Silvy felt downright clever until she remembered about that wilderness of rocks in which she was just as lost as Kel was amongst the flowers and such.

"I could tell you about some of them," she offered diffidently. "Granny was the one taught me."

Maybe that'd give him the notion that she'd appreciate more information about rocks than he'd been giving her. Maybe it wouldn't, too, seeing he was of the opinion that people ought to find things out for themselves.

"I don't mind," he said, "when we aren't too busy rock-hunting."

Whenever weren't they rock-hunting, with their noses to the ground and their hands full of specimens?

"I might could work in a few words between rocks," Silvy said in a spunky voice, "if I figured careful."

Let him make whatever he wanted out of that sassy remark.

"Just doing my thing," he muttered.

Silvy'd be glad to do hers, too, if she could ever decide just what it was. Maybe it was out somewhere, away from here, waiting for her to come looking for it. One thing she was certain sure of: Pa and Ma and Granny and the few others like them were about the last of their kind, stuck back here out of the mainstream of life. They might be able to hang onto the old ways to the end of their own lives, but Silvy'd have to take another tack with hers. She shivered.

"Rabbit jumpin' over my grave," she said soberly.

"Shiver again, so he'll jump back," Kel said.

That wasn't hard to do. It was getting downright chilly on the shady side of the slope, though that wasn't mainly what Silvy was shivering about. Pondering the future, she was shivering like one of Bet's pups going with Pa on a bear hunt the first time, scared to go and afeard to stay.

"We didn't get much for Clate today," Silvy said, "or did we?"

The garnet and a few pieces of aquamarine were all, but maybe Kel would break open one of the rocks in his knapsack and come up with something real exciting—an emerald, say, dreaming being cheap, or another piece of green amazonite like the one they had found Saturday before last over by the feldspar mine.

"Named after the Amazon River," Silvy had reported to Kel later, "though nobody ever found any there. Now why in the world would they want to call it that?"

"Does seem foolish. Maybe they just gave out of names."

It was comforting to know that even scientists that discovered things weren't always quite with it. That poet Silvy had studied in school was all mixed up about the Pacific Ocean, too—thought Cortez discovered it when it was Balboa all the time. Almost everybody used to be positive the world was flat, and a few diehards still thought so, according to Miss Henderson at school. It just went to show that what was a fact today might not turn out to be one tomorrow—which made it hard to know what to believe.

Kel walked along to within sight of the road and then turned off toward Clate's, lifting a hand in farewell.

"That right ahead of you is fetterbush," Silvy called after him. "You can tell it because the leaves have got a real high polish on them."

There were some other ways you could tell, too, same as

minerals, but likely one was all Kel could take in right now. A car was parked down by Ma's shop, and two or three people were standing outside talking to Granny. Silvy stepped along a little faster. Granny tended to get flustrated when folks began shooting questions at her.

"Psst!" Addie May stuck out her head from behind a big laurel bush. "Did you see that man followin' after you and Kel?"

"Where?"

"I wouldn't turn to look if I was you. Act like you're cutting through thisaway, and we'll trail him our own selves."

Acting like a honeybee flitting from flower to flower, though it wasn't just the season for it, Silvy sauntered off the path and joined Addie May behind the bush.

"See him dodgin' behind those trees?" Addie May asked.

By squinting a little Silvy could see a shadowy something far up the slope, moving in the direction Kel had gone.

"Has he got a gun?" Silvy asked.

"Didn't see one."

He wasn't a hunter then, and likely he wasn't the man from up on the bald, though it was hard to tell for sure about that. People with guns left them home some days. Addie May and Silvy followed him all the way to Clate's, where he peered out from behind a rosy-leafed hobblebush thicket for a while and then turned and headed back the way he had come. Silvy and Addie May just had time to scrooch down amongst the azalea bushes before he went charging past up the slope a piece, a tall man in worn jeans and high-laced boots, with a black felt hat shading his face.

"Don't reckon I'd know him again, was I to trip over him," Addie May grumbled. "What would he be wanting, I wonder?"

"That's for him to know and us to find out," Silvy said, frowning.

All of a sudden, she remembered Granny down at the cabin with folks staring at her and likely wanting to take her picture.

"Let's go!" said Silvy, and plunged down to the road with Addie May beside her.

The car was gone from out front, and Granny was sitting in one of Pa's chairs, fanning herself with her sunbonnet.

"You're back, are you?" She got up like her rheumatism was aching her and stumped up the lane. "Town gal in striped pants and a carry-around radio was asking for you, but I disremember her name. Jan, maybe? My, oh, my, I'd ruther tromp over a whole mountain any day than listen to them jabberin' young'uns!"

"How about a rock festival?" A little redhead pushed her mane of hair behind her ears. "A program to end all programs."

Silvy forgot her vow not to open her mouth except to say "yes" or "no."

"I go to a rock festival every Saturday," she said. "All day."

"You do?"

The whole program committee looked at her as though she were soft in the head instead of just making a joke. So all right; let them think so. She wasn't about to explain that her rock festivals were held at the nearest mine dump, with Kel in charge of the program.

"Hey!" said the redhead. "Somebody feed the monster."

A boy with hair almost down to his shoulders dropped money into the jukebox, which immediately began to blare out "Taking a Trip to Nowhere," accompanied by dizzily flashing lights.

The committee meeting had adjourned from school to the Hungry Bear, where all the young folks hung out—except Silvy, naturally, and the rest of the bus kids. She could hardly believe she was here now, but Jan Colby had said that, for once, everybody absolutely had to be at the meeting.

"I can't do anything with half the people not there," she had said irritably. "You can spend the night at our house."

Of course any stranger was welcome at Pa's or any other mountain home, but this was different. How could Jan tell whether Silvy would know how to act in that great big house? How could Silvy tell either, as far as that went?

"Anything you all would decide would be fine with me," Silvy had protested feebly, but Jan wouldn't take no for an answer, so here Silvy was, uneasy as a cat in a strange barn, but not about to miss anything either.

She couldn't see that the committee meeting was worth the effort. With all the talking, they hadn't come up with any ideas that made Silvy want to stand up and cheer. A speech by a retired general for Veterans Day was all, and the committee was still arguing about that.

"Who wants to listen to the same old stuff from the Establishment?" the long-haired boy complained above the sound of the jukebox. "Our heroic soldiers, etc., etc."

Silvy gave him a scorching look.

"My brother died in Vietnam," she flared in a shaking voice, "so don't you be putting him down."

She was surprised at herself, having the courage to speak up to a bunch of town kids that were supposed to know a heap more than she did. Bobby never had said was he for the war or against it. Either way, nobody'd asked him for his opinion, and he'd died doing what the government said do.

"What we're doing way off yonder minding other folks's business, I don't know," Ma had mourned. "Seems we could do better improving things right here at home."

Silvy agreed on that, but Bobby'd been a hero just the same, twice as much as though he'd been let choose whether to fight or not.

"Sorry about that," the boy said, red-faced.

"We'll have the general then," Jan said hastily, "and the following week we can give equal time to a peace speaker, OK?" She eyed the main objector. "You can be in charge of that one."

"Yeah," he said. "Yeah, I'll do that."

At the rate they were going, it was a lucky thing the committee didn't have to get up but one program every week. The principal had the say-so about the rest. Everybody began jabbering like a swarm of quarreling jays, maybe to cover up the touchy moment when Silvy had just about flown at the boy's throat.

"Look, gang," Jan said finally, "we'll be talking till midnight at this rate, so why don't we just put each one of you in charge of one program? That way, everybody'll get to have what he wants at least one time. Then we can meet once in a while to report and OK the plans. How do you all feel about that?"

Silvy knew how she felt about it. How in the world could she think up a program all by herself? She didn't know a living soul that would come and make a speech or sing a few songs or discuss something important.

"Oh, I don't think—" she began, but everybody else chimed in with "Can do" or "I guess" or "Oh, sure." Silvy's chin lifted. She wasn't going to admit she couldn't do anything the rest of them could.

"Fine!" she said, brave as a lion on the outside, shaking like jelly on the inside.

It was pride that had put her on the spot before, a spot that she was still on, too. Still, it wasn't a whole lot more trouble to fret about two things than one, and maybe if she was lucky, her program wouldn't come until late in the year.

"I want to be last," somebody said.

"No, me!"

"I couldn't touch it until after midyear exams."

There seemed to be a lot of things this crowd wanted to argue about.

"We'll do it in alphabetical order," Jan said.

The babble began again.

"First name or last name?" asked Abby Young.

"What lucky name begins with Z?"

"Mine's B. Oh, well, might as well get it over."

Silvy sighed. K wouldn't be early and wouldn't be late, though it had been too late to get her her choice of subjects from Miss Henderson.

It was after five before the committee began straggling out of the Hungry Bear. It wasn't dark here yet, but back in Curiosity Cove the sun would be hiding behind blue mountains, and evening mist would be rising on the slopes. Granny or Ma, whichever one was down at the roadside cabin, would be locking the door and starting up the lane, sniffing the wood smoke drifting down from the kitchen fire. Bugle and Bet and old Blue would come out from under the porch and start hanging around the back door, hungry for scraps from supper.

"Revenuers come hot-footin' straight to my Cousin Sam's still, like they had a map of the place." Silvy, stepping out of the Hungry Bear, would have liked to step right back in again at the sound of Lud's familiar voice. "Sam figures somebody turned him in." There Lud was, twice as big as life, sounding off to a bunch of boys on the sidewalk. "He kin spend his time in the jailhouse figurin' out who done it." Suddenly Lud saw Silvy. "Hey! What're you doin' in town? You want a ride home?"

"No," Silvy hissed. "No, thanks."

Just because she had been remembering how everything would be at home right this minute was no sign she wanted to go there. She had been invited to stay at Jan's, and that was what she was going to do. She glanced back at Jan, still chattering just inside the door. She hoped Jan hadn't heard Lud after Silvy had said so sure and certain that she didn't have any way to get home if she stayed after school. That had been the gospel truth, too, until now. Lud, who hadn't been on the bus this morning or in school either, must have come into town in his father's car for some reason.

"How're you goin' to get home then?" Lud asked.

"I'm not. I'm staying in town tonight."

"Where at? Where're you staying?"

"Silvy?" Jan came out and headed for her car. "I'm ready whenever you are."

"With her," Silvy told Lud. "See you tomorrow."

Getting into Jan's car, Silvy could see him staring after her as though she'd suddenly sprouted a second head. An extra would come in handy, too, with all the thinking she'd better be doing about this program and about how to get to college in case she decided to take her foot in her hand and head for the far horizon. She just wished the matter had never come up, but she couldn't blame anybody for that except herself, talking biggety when she should have said nothing and very little of that.

For just a minute, riding up the drive to the Colbys' house, which looked twice as big close to as it did just going by on the bus, Silvy almost wished she had gone on home with Lud. Likely she'd do a million things wrong and never know she had. Still, if she watched carefully and didn't talk much, it didn't seem she could make a whole lot of mistakes. Carrying Ma's covered basket for her overnight things, Silvy tagged along behind Jan, who left the car in the garage and said, "We'll go in the front. Daisy'll murder anybody that comes through the kitchen when she's cooking dinner."

A cook then. Silvy lagged behind. This was going to be too grand for her—that she knew. Jan ushered her into a huge living room with furniture like pictures of places that Silvy had seen on TV.

"Mama, this is Silvy Kershaw," Jan announced to a small woman with her graying hair done in a swirl on top of her head. "My mother."

"So nice you could come," said Mrs. Colby. "Jan has been telling me about you."

That was just manners because the only thing Jan could have told was that Silvy was a poor mountain girl that couldn't even get a ride home from town. Silvy rummaged in her basket.

"Ma hopes you can use this. It's from our own bee gums."

In this big beautiful room, Ma's sourwood honey didn't look like anything much, though Granny had fixed a little cornhusk cover around the jar, tied up with a piece of orange yarn to pretty it up some. Mrs. Colby, though, made out it was the greatest thing on earth.

"Why, thank you!" For all she was so stylish and lived in this elaborate house, she didn't talk the least bit standoffish. "Sourwood, isn't it, my favorite of all. Please thank your mother for me."

"Yes, ma'am."

Silvy looked warily around her. There seemed to be a lot of things she could knock over in case her foot got bogged down in the deep carpet. The worst were a couple of little spindle-legged tables with old-timey ladies on them, every bit done in china right down to the lace edging on their dresses. The best thing would be to sit down out of harm's way, though the gold-and-white brocade chairs looked too fine for mere sitting.

"You have a nice place," said Silvy.

It was hard to know just what to say, but you couldn't make a mistake praising folks's things. Mrs. Colby looked around the room.

"French Provincial," she said. "Jan doesn't care for it, but—"

"It suits you, ma'am," said Silvy, still rooted to the spot with the carrying basket in her hand.

Jan cut in impatiently.

"It isn't the now thing," she told her mother. "That you'll have to admit."

Silvy wasn't the now thing either, not by a long shot. Jan should see the Kershaw place in Curiosity Cove if she had so much fault to find with her own. Just thinking of Jan out home gave Silvy a skittery feeling like the time she'd swallowed a spider by mistake. With no way to repay, she never should have come. It was curiosity that had brought her and guilt at never being able to attend committee meetings after school. For a panicky moment, she felt like darting across the pale green carpet and out the door, but with Lud and the school bus long gone, about all she could do was to stick it out. Besides, she might never have a chance to see inside a place like this again, so she'd best make the most of it.

"You might show Silvy where to leave her things," Mrs. Colby said. "Early dinner tonight because your father has to go out to a meeting."

Silvy's things weren't many, mostly clean clothes for school tomorrow, and, naturally, her homework, which was a report on some of the minerals she and Kel had found. She didn't know what she'd do for lunch tomorrow, but likely Addie May'd have a bite to spare. Silvy just hoped she wouldn't be sleeping in the same room with Jan, who'd be sure to have a lot of fancy clothes, but even that would give Silvy a chance to see how town folks lived. What she had to bear in mind was that this was research, like for her term paper, and not a way of making Silverbell Kershaw look like somebody she wasn't.

"In here." Jan, with her transistor in her hand again, pushed open the door of a bedroom that was even prettier than the downstairs, if possible—mostly blue with touches of sunshine yellow. "Your bath's in there." A bath all her own—Silvy had really fallen into a tub of honey! Jan hesitated in the doorway. "I'm right next if you want anything."

"Oh, I won't! I mean, it's lovely." Silvy had worked out a few things she'd say so as not to sound as though she'd never set foot out of Curiosity Cove in all her life. "I think it's so exciting, you planning to be an airline hostess."

"Oh, that! I had to say something. Keeps the teacher happy."

"You don't want to?"

Jan plunked herself down on a little chair flounced in a yellow poppy print.

"I don't know *what* I want," she said.

"You're not the only one," said Silvy.

The difference was that even if she did know, she probably couldn't do it, while Jan could afford anything she took a notion to.

"All the parents can think about is college," Jan said, "but that's not my thing. At least, I don't think it is." She scowled. "I'd like to be—oh, free, you know?"

Silvy didn't, really, though there was a lot of talk about it on TV from young people who went out and lived in communes at the end of nowhere—which was a fair description of Curiosity Cove, too. It seemed peculiar, Silvy with a notion to get out, and the others who were already out wanting to get in. She just didn't understand it, but there were a lot of things she didn't understand. That was another reason for trying to get more schooling to help her hunt for some answers.

One thing she especially didn't understand was why Jan Colby, who had been homecoming queen and on the Student Council and in half a dozen school clubs, would be sitting down talking to Silvy about her feelings, as though Silvy could give her some advice instead of the other way around.

"It's hard to decide," said Silvy. "There's so much—" She hesitated, trying for the right words. "So much of the world a person can't hardly decide where to grab a-holt."

Oh, dear, here she was talking mountainy when she'd vowed to be real careful! That was what came of trying to think and talk at the same time.

"I'd let go of most of it if I had my choice," Jan said. "I don't do all this stuff because I want to. It's for the image, my father being a banker and civic leader and all that." Her lip curled. "You ought to do things because you feel right about them, not so you'll look good to the public. What I think is, the older generation are a bunch of hypocrites!"

Oh, my! Jan really was in a snarl with herself.

"You may be right," said Silvy, giving the soft answer that was supposed to turn away wrath.

She didn't think that what Jan said applied to Ma and Pa and Granny, who were what they were and probably had never even heard tell of an image.

"Oh, well." Jan's thoughtful mood disappeared as fast as it had come. She jumped up and headed for her own room. "I'll go wash my hands. Mama'll be calling us for dinner pretty soon."

Silvy, alone in this pretty room, took a long look at herself in the tall mirror—a little fair-haired girl in a blue dress, about as outstanding in a wilderness of blue carpet as one of the rocks that Kel tossed back on the heap. So what did she expect? To shine out like one of Clate's gemstones?

"Ready, girls!" Mrs. Colby called.

Silvy, a little behindhand with her face-washing and hair-brushing on account of having taken so long to explore her bedroom, joined Jan at the top of the curving stairway. She looked down on the top of Mr. Colby's head, with his hair carefully draped over a thin spot. Pa had all his hair still, but of course he didn't have to worry himself to death about everybody's money. Besides, Pa might be younger. Silvy had never thought much about Pa's age. He was just there, like rocks and mountains.

"And what about you, young lady?" Mr. Colby said at dinner as Silvy sat looking sideways at Jan to see if the smaller fork was for the salad or should be saved for pie, in case they had any. "Will you be off to college next year?"

"Oh, you'd approve of her!" Jan said. "She's going to be a teacher."

Imagine Jan remembering that from back the first day of school before Miss Henderson divided the class and shooed Silvy back into the mountains for the rest of the year! It just proved that a person had better be extra careful about talking without doing a lot of thinking first.

"What college do you have in mind?" Mr. Colby asked.

"I haven't made my pick yet," said Silvy. What was the name of the college with the work program that the librarian had mentioned that day and that Silvy had never gone back to see about? Greenwood? Hillside? "Highcliff, maybe."

That was about the biggest maybe ever known, but miracles did happen—not that Silvy had any solid evidence. What would be a real, true miracle would be for her to head herself once and for all in a definite direction. That was the way Kel did, like a missile on automatic guidance. It could be he'd never get where he wanted to go, but anyway he had a clear destination in mind, so he didn't have to use up all his energy trying to decide which way to jump.

"Better get your application in," Mr. Colby advised.

In his world getting the application in was the main problem, not money. Wouldn't he be struck dumb if Silvy were to speak up and tell him she had nine dollars and some cents in his high-toned bank and not the first idea how to get any more?

"I keep telling Jan to get with it," Mr. Colby went on, "but she's not— She's undecided."

"I'm not undecided," Jan said in a stubborn voice. "I'm just not going."

Silvy pretended great interest in her pork chop, which this Daisy that murdered people for walking through her kitchen had fixed up real tasty with mushroom gravy.

"Now, Jan," Mrs. Colby said nervously, "we can talk this over some other time."

Jan muttered something about there not being anything to talk over, and Silvy started babbling about the first thing that popped into her head.

"My section at school is doing Appalachian Studies this year," she said. "Everybody picks a different subject."

Mr. Colby grabbed onto that before Silvy hardly got the words out of her mouth.

"And what's your topic?"

"Rocks." Silvy caught herself just before she absent-mindedly picked up the pork chop to gnaw off the last little scraps of meat. That wasn't how people did that could afford to waste a bite here and there. "Kel McLeod and I are doing it together because it's too much for one."

And because Mary Ellerbe had walked off with Silvy's topic. Mr. and Mrs. Colby both chimed in then, asking what kind of luck they were having and where did they go to look and was there any special kind of rock they were interested in. Silvy reluctantly laid down her fork. If she had to talk, naturally she couldn't eat.

"We've found some things," she said. "Gems for Clate Fowler and some other minerals that Kel likes better. He's going to be a mineralogist." She had to stop for breath, but if she didn't stop too long, she'd get back to that pork chop yet. "Samarskite, Kel's found, and columbite and euxenite."

"In the mine dumps?" Mr. Colby asked.

"Some, and some up by a slide on the bald and some back of Kel's where his pa blasted out some rock."

"You're planning some kind of exhibit of these minerals?"

"Not that I've heard. Just reports for class."

"Your friend ought to talk to the people at the feldspar mine. They're always trying for ways to extract more minerals from the ore—wring the last bit of value out of the rock."

"Like killing hogs," Silvy said. "Pa kin—can—use every bit but the squeal."

She closed her mouth a dozen words too late. Killing hogs wasn't anything to talk about here in this delicate room, with its silver and crystal and linen—not that Silvy was ever let stay around at hog-killing time, anyway.

"This's no place for a little young girl," Granny would say. "Run on over and talk to Addie May."

Silvy was always glad enough to go, though seeing she ate the meat, it seemed only fair she should help get it ready.

"There'll be plenty for you to do afterward," Ma said, "grinding up the scraps for sausage."

Silvy didn't much fancy that either, but with Granny flinging in the spices and herbs, the Kershaws had the best sausage anywhere around. On TV, Farmer Green's sausage came sizzling to the table all ready to eat, with it never crossing most folks's minds that real people had to figure out how to make it look and taste so good. That was another thing that was different about Curiosity Cove: people made most things their own selves instead of running to the store for stuff already fixed.

"Just the same," said Jan, probably afraid that Silvy would go on talking about hog-killing, "I'd like to have a rock festival."

Silvy gratefully turned her attention back to the pork chop. There was no need for her to comment on rock festivals, which she didn't know anything about except on TV. Besides, Mr. Colby had plenty to say.

"A rock festival?" He gave Jan a suspicious look. "You mean music, so-called? With drugs, no doubt. That's *all* we need around here!"

"Just a program for school," Jan said soothingly, but there was a speculative gleam in her eye. "Now that you mention it, though—"

"I didn't mention it!" He eyed his daughter with alarm. "And see that you don't again either. It'd put the bank in a bad light for you—"

Jan laid down her fork.

"And we can't have the bank put in a bad light, can we? What's for dessert?"

"Chocolate cream pie." Mrs. Colby turned to Silvy. "I hope you like it."

"Oh, yes, ma'am!"

Silvy had never had any, but she had seen pictures. Ma leaned more to apple, blueberry, blackberry, and wild strawberry—whatever was ripe in the uplands or along the forest roads. Silvy glanced in Jan's direction. The meal was nearly over, and she still had the same pieces of silverware left as Jan. It just went to show that if she kept her eyes open, it wasn't so hard to do things right. Truth to tell, though, she'd just as soon be back home where she didn't feel as though she were sitting on a keg of dynamite that might explode any minute. There was still plenty of time to say the wrong thing or eat with her spoon when it should be a fork or for Jan and her folks to argue some more—sort of submarine arguing that didn't come quite to the surface. Anyway, the pie was good—rich and chocolaty and topped with two inches of fluffy meringue.

"This's purely delicious, ma'am."

Ma always liked to hear when the food was good, and probably Mrs. Colby did, too, though in this case she couldn't take any of the credit. Mr. Colby stood up.

"Sorry to rush off, people, but the meeting's called for seven-thirty. Back early, I hope." He brushed his wife's cheek with a kiss. "Have fun, kids. Nice to have met you, Silvy. Good luck with the rocks."

Silvy supposed it wouldn't be right to offer to help clear up unless Jan did. Besides, it'd be easy to knock over one of the crystal goblets that Silvy hadn't even dared drink out of during the whole meal.

"I like it out at your place," Jan said when she and Silvy were settled in what Jan called the family room, with their homework spread out on a big round table and a tall stack of records playing a good bit too loud.

"We don't live where you talked to Granny," Silvy said. "That's just to sell things out of. Our house is up on the ridge."

That and the barn and the pigpen and a few other weathered buildings that looked a hundred years old. Silvy gave Jan a thoughtful look. Jan didn't need to go to all that trouble to brag on Silvy's place, though she didn't seem to be the type for soft-talking people.

"And your grandmother's a doll!"

Jan's mother was more what Silvy would call a doll, soft

and fluffy and dressed up pretty like the ones in the big Wish Book that came at Christmas for Ma to buy from in case she had any cash to spare. Granny was more on the order of the pioneer woman that Silvy had read about in her history book, toughened up from hard work, browned by the sun and the wind, wiry from tramping around mountains all her life.

"A cornhusk doll," Silvy said.

Jan sat with her chin in her hands, staring at nothing that Silvy could see.

"You'll go a far piece to find a place as pretty as you've got right here," Silvy said, "and I thank you for asking me."

Thanks would be all Jan would get because there wasn't a way in the world Silvy could repay her. Let it be a lesson to her for getting herself beholden just for curiosity's sake! By rights Silvy should ask Jan out to her place, but it'd be downright humiliating if Jan came out and saw how plain Silvy lived.

"I might come and stay with you some weekend," Jan said, "if you don't mind."

Silvy's heart sank down to the soles of her shoes, but no Kershaw ever turned anybody away from the door.

"You're welcome," she said, flustrated as an aspen in a high wind. "Take us as you find us."

"We'll soon know." With the tweezers Kel laid a scrap of grayish rock embedded with red-brown grains on a little block of charcoal on Clate Fowler's worktable. "Toss me the book again, Silvy."

Silvy stared drearily out at rain pouring down the windows of Clate's shop when she should have been gluing rock specimens onto a mineral card. She passed Kel the field book, which he flipped open.

"Let's see. Won't melt on the charcoal but turns gray."

He lit the Bunsen burner that he and Clate had set up like the one in the chemistry lab at school except that this one ran on bottled gas. Then he picked up the blowpipe, a curved metal tube, and, with his cheeks puffed out, blew steadily across the flame, which touched the charcoal and the piece of whatever it was.

"Infusible, right. Gray, right. The sulfuric acid, Silvy."

"Yes, sir," said Silvy. "Right away, sir."

The chemical shelf was lined with things that Kel and Clate called reagents—several kinds of acid in small bottles, ethyl alcohol, borax, sodium carbonate. Silvy didn't even try to understand what the two of them were doing, Kel more than Clate, who was too busy working on gemstones and jewelry to run chemical tests on the offbeat minerals that Kel was so partial to.

Kel put down the blowpipe and dripped a tiny bit of sulfuric acid through an eyedropper onto the mineral. A bluish-green flame flickered for a moment on the specimen and disappeared.

"Just what I thought," Kel said in satisfaction. "Monazite."

"Great," Silvy said languidly.

She fished a piece of feldspar out of a divided tray and glued it next to a scrap of mica on the mineral card. Clate sold the cards with their dozen or so specimens to the outlanders who were more curious than serious about rocks.

"Good souvenirs," he said, "and not too dear."

Silvy, as usual, would just as lief be home doing something else—helping Granny make cornhusk dolls for their own shop or knitting a little on the mittens and caps that they sometimes sold to the few winter travelers. Kel, though, said this was a good way for her to learn how to tell the minerals apart.

"Mica, feldspar, garnet, fool's gold," she chanted under her breath, putting each one above its printed label on the card. Monazite—she had her mouth open to ask Kel why it was called that, but likely he wouldn't know, or if he did, he'd tell her to look it up. Samarskite and monazite sounded as though they belonged together, like ham hocks and greens.

"How many 've you got now?" Clate asked.

It was quiet in here today, with the tumbler banished to the shed, where it made only a distant rumble as it slid the stones over and over to give them a high polish.

"Ten." Silvy counted the completed cards on the table.

Twelve-fifty for Clate whenever he sold them, after which he would give Kel and Silvy something for their work. Clate wasn't asking about the cards, though.

"Samarskite, columbite, euxenite, monazite," Kel said, "and—"

"And beryl, aquamarine, garnet, and autunite," Silvy put in.

"No, no, not those. They don't count."

"Why don't they count?" Silvy asked. "We found them, didn't we?"

"This is a special group," Kel said. "What we need now are allanite, uraninite, though there should have been some of that in with that autunite we found—" He counted on his fingers. "Clarkeite, cyrtolite, and pyrochlore. Those we know for sure are around here and maybe some others if we can find out where."

This was a big burst of talk for Kel, although he wasn't talking to Silvy but to Clate, who might be getting the message, as Silvy wasn't. With a stub of pencil, she wrote down all the names she could remember on the torn-off corner of an old newspaper. Allanite, clarkeite, and uraninite weren't so bad, but Silvy, though she had always been a good speller, had to guess on the other two that Kel had mentioned.

She spent a lot of time looking things up, either in the field guide or in the school library during noon hour. Mostly she just looked up where the names came from. Sometimes they were from the places where the minerals were found (autunite from Autun, France), sometimes from the men who discovered or classified them (allanite would be one of those and probably clarkeite, too), sometimes from the color (aquamarine from *aqua marina*, sea water), sometimes from other characteristics, like pegmatite from a Greek word *pegma*, which meant stuck together, as pegmatite certainly was, all full of a lot of different minerals.

"That batch of stones in the tumbler could come out about now." Clate got up slow and painful and headed for the shed.

"I could get them for you," Silvy said eagerly.

She was tired of gluing things, and, besides, the stones always looked so pretty when they came out of the tumbler that it was hard to believe they were the same rough pieces Clate had started with. It was almost magic, like the dogwood in the spring popping out of what looked like old dead branches.

Kel hardly even looked up from his work. Except for the gemstones that Clate used, the minerals Kel and Silvy found never went into the tumbler but instead were analyzed and labeled and put carefully away. Kel always kept them at Clate's, probably so his brothers at home couldn't get their hands on them.

"You can help," Clate told Silvy, though without a lot of enthusiasm.

He was mighty particular about how the stones were handled. First of all, the tumbler had to run just so fast and no faster so the stones would slide easy against each other instead of banging together and getting chipped and broken. The mixture of water and abrasives for the first and second grinds had to be exactly right, and with the final polishing Clate got downright persnickety, trying this and that and the other along with the chemical polishing agent. Scraps of sole leather, ground nutshells, sawdust, wooden pegs—Clate always tossed one or the other of them into the tumbler to see which would bring the stones to the highest shine.

"Flip the switch, please," Clate said.

The drum, which had been revolving on a set of rollers, pulleys, and belts, eased to a stop. Clate took off the lid and fished out a handful of polished stones.

"Seems all right," he said after a careful look.

In some ways, Kel and Clate were two of a kind, never the least bit wrought up, though Silvy could hardly take her eyes off the glimmering stones, which Clate would make into necklaces, bracelets, and earrings. Kel might have it in mind to be a mineralogist, but Silvy didn't think it was half as exciting as what Clate was doing, making pretty things out of rocks that a person might walk right over without having any idea how beautiful they might be.

"May I sort them for you?" Silvy asked.

"By color will be best this time," he said. "This is a mixed lot—beryl and quartz, green apatite, a little unakite, and some others."

Silvy and Kel had found some of it in the mine dumps, but a good share of the quartz Clate had bought from a place that supplied rough stones to people that wanted them. With Clate hobbling along behind, Silvy carried the stones carefully back into the shop in a cardboard box.

"The cerium oxide's working out the best for the final polishing," Clate told Kel, "plus some sole leather."

"Cerium oxide?" Kel set down the blowpipe, which made him look like a fire-breathing dragon, and turned off the Bunsen burner.

"Thought you might be interested," Clate said.

"I am. Just another use for the—"

Silvy made a mental note to look up cerium, which must be something important to make Kel quit what he was doing, even for a minute. Otherwise, Silvy didn't pay him and Clate much mind. She was too fascinated with the stones spread out on the table. They didn't sparkle like the ones that Clate faceted, but they shimmered and shone like the satin kimono that Silvy's brother Bobby had sent home from Vietnam with flowers embroidered in silk on the back. Silvy spread out the stones—red, brown, green, gold, milky white, and even a few striped in different colors. The colors put her in mind of flowers—goldenrod, asters, laurel, even hearts-bustin'-with-love. If she arranged them right, they even looked like flowers—a stone for each petal, some bits of green for the leaves. Smiling, Silvy put down a brown stone that looked for all the world like a hovering bee if she squinched her eyes up a little.

"It's stopped raining," said Kel. "Let's go."

"Where?" Silvy didn't much want to wade around through a lot of damp bushes. Besides, she had been so taken up with arranging the gemstones like a bouquet of flowers that she hadn't sorted them the way Clate asked her. "I ought to finish these first."

"No rush." Clate looked up from the piece of rose quartz he was cementing into a dangling earring. "What you got there?"

"Nothing much," said Silvy. "Just the colors are so pretty, like flowers."

If she could glue them onto something, they'd make a real nice picture she could hang on her wall when it was all snow outside, to remind herself that spring would be back as sure as the sun came up in the morning.

Clate gave her a studying look.

"I've got some stones that were damaged in the tumbler," he said. "Take 'em home if you want."

"I do thank you," Silvy said gravely.

She didn't have a whole lot of time to run gemstones through her fingers like a princess in a made-up story, but it'd give her a real rich feeling. Somehow or other, she'd make herself a picture, too, if only to prove she could.

"I'll have to stop at home to get some different shoes," Silvy told Kel, "and to drop off my gemstones."

"I was thinking we might prospect around your pa's place anyway," Kel said, "if it wouldn't put him out any."

"He won't mind," Silvy said, "especially if we find a handful of diamonds back of the barn."

"Don't count on it, but I figure that vein might—"

Vein of what? Mighty nigh everything around was rock, so Silvy didn't see how Kel was going to divide it up into veins. He left the sentence dangling as he went out the door with the battered knapsack that he carried with him everywhere he went.

"See you next Saturday," Silvy called back to Clate, "and thanks again for the gemstones." She glanced down toward the road. "Who's that yonder?"

"Couldn't say," said Kel.

Lots of people came to look at Clate's rocks. This one, a tall man in khaki clothes, sloshed up the path.

"Nice day," he said, looking sharp at Kel and Silvy as he passed.

A nice day if he'd never seen a better, but it was something to say.

"Yes, sir," Kel said.

Silvy turned to look at the man just as he turned to look at her. He'd know her—and Kel, too—the next time he saw them.

"Looks like rain, though," Silvy said, and skittered after Kel. "It might could be," she muttered.

"Might could be what?"

"Him. The man that was followin' us that day. Addie May and I watched him."

Kel simply stared. Like as not, Silvy had forgotten to tell him, with all the excitement of going to stay at Jan's right after.

"He's not wearing the same hat, but—" Silvy turned to look again, but Clate's door was closing behind the visitor. "Some folks 've got more than one hat, I guess."

"No law against walking around," Kel said when Silvy had told him the story, which didn't sound so almighty mysterious as it had seemed at the time. "We do it our own selves."

"He was sneaking," Silvy said.

"Some folks do that way. A blockader, maybe."

Blockaders! To hear folks talk you'd think there was one behind every bush.

"Figuring to sell Clate a jug? No, it was you he was watching."

Kel's lips twitched.

"Folks don't get to see a handsome young fellow like me every day in the week."

"Some're lucky and some aren't," said Silvy. "Hard to tell which is which."

Kel was only fooling, naturally, but the truth was he wasn't bad-looking when something struck him funny or when he found a special kind of rock or when he identified a mineral that he hadn't been sure of before. Then his lips quirked up at the corners and his dark eyes sparkled, with a little glint in them like some of the gemstones when a person looked real close.

Down by the road, Granny, with her old brown shawl around her shoulders, was rocking and knitting on the little stoop where some watery sunshine hit her. This time of year Silvy favored putting up a sign, *Sound Horn for Service*. On a damp day like this and with the bright leaves nearly gone off the trees, there wouldn't be many people on the road. Granny wouldn't hear of closing up, though.

"No reason I can't set down there and knit or work on the doll babies," she said. "I got nothin' else to fill my time—old wore-out granny-woman, no good to ary livin' soul."

In gloomy weather Granny tended to get gloomy to match, with a lot of talk about being useless and just as well off dead. She always waited, though, for Silvy and Ma to say, "Now, Granny! What ever would we do without you?" or "Law, we'd be purely lost. Nobody can make the cornhusk dolls or foller the quilt pattern like you."

Silvy guessed this was just part of being old, like rheumatics gnawing on the joints. Likely she'd need a sight of cheering up her own self if she didn't die young, exhausted from trying to decide what she wanted her life to be like and how to make it be that way once she did decide.

"Sold three of them cornhusk babies," Granny said gleefully. "Folks'd been figurin' on ridin' the parkway, only it's fogged in like the inside of a feather tick. No cloud without a silver lining—for somebody." She peered at Silvy's cardboard box. "What've you got in there?"

"Gems!" said Silvy. "Like for kings and such." She opened the box. "I won't charge you a cent to look, either."

Granny peered in.

"My, oh, my! Kelsey, if this here's what you're a-diggin' up, you're goin' to end up rich as plum puddin'."

Kel mumbled something that Silvy didn't catch, but he smiled at Granny.

"That'll be the year they have two Christmases," he said.

To him, gemstones were just a way to earn a few dollars and to help Clate out until he could do his own hunting. It was samarskite and the others that took Kel's fancy, though for the life of her Silvy couldn't tell why, except that they'd help make him a mineralogist. She had looked that up, too—somebody that studied minerals, the dictionary said, which was no big surprise. The encyclopedia embroidered it up some, going on about how mineralogy included chemistry, physics, geology, crystallography, geography, and something called the economic side, which dealt with mining methods, ways to separate the metals

99

from the ores, and developing uses for minerals once they finally were separated.

"Jan's father said the people at the feldspar mine are working on some new things," Silvy told Kel as they walked up to the house, with Bugle and old Blue wagging along behind.

"What new things?"

"New ways of doing," Silvy said vaguely. "How to get more minerals out of the ore and not throw away so much."

Talking about Mr. Colby made her think about Jan, which she'd just as soon not do. Whenever Silvy saw her, which wasn't often, Jan mentioned coming out to Silvy's place to stay the night, but so far she hadn't done it. Silvy felt relieved about that but also ashamed of feeling that way. Being beholden to somebody was a weight on her mind, like saying she was going to do something when she didn't have the first idea how.

"Come any time you're a mind to," Silvy had finally said.

That way it was all up to Jan whether she came or didn't. Likely she had changed her mind about it, anyway. It could have been a sudden notion that had made her ask, or maybe she was just knocking herself out to be friendly. Silvy had just about worn out her brain trying to think of ways to amuse Jan if she ever did come. Maybe a visit to Clate's shop or—

"She might like to hunt rocks with us," Silvy said timidly to Kel.

"Who?"

Kel took a sharp look at a boulder alongside the lane but passed it by.

"Jan Colby, if she comes to visit."

"Wouldn't mind," said Kel.

One thing it'd do for sure. It'd cure Jan of coming out

here again if she ruined her shoes and her good clothes clawing through rock piles and maybe losing hold of the transistor radio that she hardly moved a step without.

"Will you step inside?" Silvy said. "I want to put my gemstones away."

"I'll just prospect around out here some," Kel said. "It was dusky dark the last time I—" His mouth hung open and his ears turned bright red as Silvy pounced on his words.

"So it was you, was it? Pa *said* it was a real uncommon bear that wore shoes. Why'd you run off thataway, I'd like to know."

"People get itchy trigger fingers when folks 're prowling around in the nighttime. I was hunting rocks up the slope a piece and headed for home thisaway. I'd a-sung out going by the door, but I was looking at rocks and fell over that plow." He grinned. "Scared myself almost worse'n your pa's gun would of. You going to tell him?"

Silvy considered.

"Can't see why I should. He decided it was a blockader anyway soon's he figured out it wasn't a bear. Psst! There he is!" Pa, looking like a thundercloud, came out of the barn. "All right if Kel and I look for rocks around here?"

"Shouldn't be no trouble findin' 'em—hard to find ary thing else. Howdy, Kelsey. You handy with auto engines? Can't get this plaguey thing started."

"Where're you going, Pa?" Silvy wouldn't mind a trip into town if that was where he was bound for.

"Nowhere," Pa said, "even if I get 'er started. I got all these black walnuts to husk."

The way Pa got the hulls off the walnuts was to drive the car back and forth over them on the rocky lane or the barn floor. In a way, it was easier on the hands than whacking the husks with clubs and then picking the remains off with fingers that got stained brown in no time. Worst of all, they stayed that way for weeks.

"I'll take a look," said Kel. "You figure it's starter trouble?"

"Won't start, is all I know," Pa said. "Give me a good mule every time. Leastways, it goes."

"If it feels like it. It could tromp out those hulls with its hoofs, too," Silvy said.

She sounded a little sassier than she meant to but not a bit sassier than she felt. It did seem Pa might try to talk up to date instead of carrying on about mules as though he'd think nothing of hitching one to a wagon and driving into town like in the old days.

"None of your lip, girl!" Pa said.

Silvy didn't take that much to heart. Pa was like old Blue, not as cross as a person'd think from the sound of him. Kel and Pa disappeared into the barn, and Silvy carried her gemstones into the kitchen and grabbed her old shoes from behind the stove. Ma wasn't there—maybe over talking to Addie May's ma—but some quilt pieces were laid out in a pattern on the table, ready to be put together.

Outside again, Silvy took Kel's prospector's pick out of the knapsack and amused herself by prying pieces of rock off where Pa had whittled down the side of the hill once to make a turnaround for the car at the top of the lane. She didn't expect to find anything special or recognize it if she did, but it'd be good practice.

Nothing, nothing, nothing, but at least she was accumulating a nice little batch of specimens for Kel to check over whenever he and Pa got through muttering and mumbling in the barn. Then—Silvy's eyes widened.

"Kel!" she yelled. "Kel! I found something! Prettiest rock you ever saw!"

8

"Ain't lost my eye yit!" Pa took aim with the .22 at a green cluster of mistletoe high up in a big old red maple, almost bare of its scarlet leaves. The rifle cracked, and the mistletoe, big as a bushel basket, swooshed down to the ground. "To shoot 'em down, you got to clip 'em off right at the stem. A man don't need to shoot quite that good for bear, but it keeps you keen for gray squirrel."

Jan Colby, blue-jeaned and wide-eyed, watched Pa with a fascinated expression. Beside her, leaning against a boulder, her ever-present transistor was muttering "Hannibal Square" under its breath.

"Wouldn't it be easier just to climb up and snip it off?" she asked.

"Now wouldn't I be a sight out there on one of them spindly little branches, like a bobcat swingin' on a cobweb?" Pa said. "Those limbs wouldn't even hold up Silverbell, little as she is."

Pa was being real mannerly to Jan, though he was in an almighty rush. He was going bear-hunting up in the high country with Kel's father and Addie May's and maybe Lud's and one or two others, along with the feldspar company's doctor from town. He was let come partly on account of having sewed Addie May's pa's hand up so good when it got mangled in the crusher a few years back.

Pa quickly shot down a dozen more clumps of mistletoe, and Silvy ran out to pick them up in Ma's washbasket and carry them up to the house. The waxy yellow-white berries were nice and plump, pretty as they'd ever be and sure to please the flower-store man in town. Ma and Granny had been out gathering galax leaves, which were bronzy now, and all the bittersweet they could find to make up a good load for when Addie May's Cousin Juny came after it in his pickup truck this afternoon.

"Don't know as I ever noticed it much," Kel had said when Silvy, educating him on plants the same as he was supposed to be teaching her about rocks, told him all about galax on one of their prospecting trips.

And him born and brought up right around here too! It just went to show that he saw only what he wanted to see and walked right past everything else without even noticing. Silvy couldn't fault him so much for that, though. She had always been the same way with rocks, preferring to look at the growing things that made more of a show of themselves.

Silvy ought to be out right now looking for more galax —another good reason she'd just as lief Jan hadn't taken a notion to come visiting this weekend.

"If it's perfectly convenient," she had said, polite as could be.

"Anytime's fine," Silvy had said.

That was overstating the fact by a good lot, but in a way it would be a relief to have the visit over and her debts paid. It was mighty like swallowing some of the concoctions Granny whipped up to cure something Silvy hadn't even gotten yet. The more Silvy thought it over, the harder it always was to get the tonic down.

Besides, Jan might as well find out sooner as later that mountain ways weren't like life in town in any way, shape, or form—no fancy furniture, deep carpets, fine silver or china. Silvy wasn't about to apologize for anything, though. It was Jan's turn to feel out of place if anybody was going to.

"That do you?" Pa pushed his hunting cap to the back of his head. "I got to get movin'. Time we get up to the camp and settled in, it'll be dusky dark." With the girls trailing behind him, he walked up to the house and began readying his gear for the bear hunt—rifle, shells, fire-blackened old coffeepot, blanket. "Where're my rations?"

"Right here." Ma handed a bulging poke out the back door. "Cold biscuit, potatoes, carrots, a chunk of cured meat—"

"Meat!" Pa said. "Woman, it's meat we're a-goin' after. You got no faith in us gettin' anyways a squirrel or two right off?"

"Mighty hard shootin' squirrel in the dead of night," she said briskly. "This's for tonight's supper." Her eyes glinted with amusement. "Tomorrow you won't be needin' it, with all that bear meat you're countin' on so strong."

Pa gave her a slow grin.

"Never you mind!" he said. "You just get that big old iron kettle ready and the water a-bilin'."

"You *boil* bear meat?" Jan asked, hypnotized either by Pa or by "Answer Me That" from the transistor.

"Set, will you!" Pa roared at Bugle, Bet, and old Blue, who were milling around as though they'd caught the scent of bear already. "You'll get plenty exercise before you're done." He turned to Jan. "They're special bred for bear, bold and severe—cain't hardly wait to go." He paused. "What you do with bear meat, you get you some medium-sized rocks about like potatoes and drop 'em into a pot of bilin' water along with the meat."

"Rocks?" Jan asked doubtfully.

"Yup. Any old kind'll do. Bile 'em all together for five-six hours." He let the punch line hang fire for a second. "Then toss the meat away and eat the rocks."

Jan burst into giggles.

"With mustard and relish. I can taste them now."

"I'm on my way." Pa picked up his gear and, loaded like a mule, whistled to the dogs and headed down the lane. Addie May's pa, whose car was running right then ("Downhill all the time," Addie May said, "and uphill sometimes"), would pick him up, dogs and all. "Back when you see me."

"Did you ever go bear-hunting?" Jan turned her transistor up a little louder and set it down beside the mountain of mistletoe on the ground.

"Me? No, nor any other female, either," said Silvy, horrified. "That's for the menfolks, and even they're a-draggin' when they get home."

Let's see now. What next to fill in the time? It was the luckiest thing in the world that Jan hadn't come out until this morning, driving her own little car, and that Pa had been shooting down mistletoe for the last two hours. This afternoon Kel would take them both rock-hunting, and tomorrow or maybe even today they'd stop by Clate's shop just to look. That still left some gaps that Silvy'd have to fill in somehow or other, but maybe Jan would go home early Sunday afternoon. Maybe she wouldn't, too, but it wasn't mannerly to ask.

"Right here," said Silvy, "is where I found the thulite."

Jan looked around at what seemed like a plain, ordinary outcropping of rock if a person didn't know any better.

"Thulite? What's that?"

"It's a mineral—rosy pink like flowers."

Mixed up with the white feldspar that it came in, it put Silvy in mind of the laurel-that-Granny-called-ivy that folks came from miles around to see in the springtime.

Kel, probably outdone from trying to get Pa's car started, hadn't been much fired up about the thulite the day Silvy'd found it here by the turnaround. His ideas had changed, though, when he'd prospected around some himself and found a specimen of what he thought might be allanite, another of the dreary-looking minerals that he always preferred. Muttering about thorium, cerium, and erbium as though he were saying a charm against witches, he had worked until dark, finding a few more scraps of the pink thulite for Silvy, too.

"Thulite's a kind of zoisite, it says here," Kel had read from the old field guide, which was growing more battered by the day. "S'posed to be fluorescent if we had an ultraviolet light to see it by. Allanite, though, if this is it—" He held out a hunk of rock with some skinny crystals in it. "That's radioactive—have to put a Geiger counter on it at school to make sure. Looks right, though—dark brown color, pitchy luster, red stain in the feldspar around the crystal grains and cracks radiating out, just like in the book."

Silvy would likely be a bearcat at identifying minerals, too, if she had a book to do it by and pictures besides. There weren't any pictures of her thulite, which was eight times prettier than the allanite. Clate, at least, had been real pleased and had put the thulite and feldspar into the tumbler, promising to give Silvy some of it back whenever it was polished up right, besides paying for what he used himself. She was saving a special spot for it in the flower picture she was making out of the gemstones he had given her. She had them laid out like a bouquet on a piece of heavy canvas stretched tight over a wooden frame and kept moving them around like pieces on a checkerboard till she could get them looking just right.

Besides the thulite that she had to wait on before she could add some pink and white flowers to the yellow, blue, and red, she needed some more green for the leaves. Clate might be able to cut some stems for her on his trim saw, though it'd be picky work, and likely some pieces of Granny's green yarn would do about as well. Then she could glue everything down and her picture would be done.

"Come set!" Ma called. "Dinner's on!"

It'd be lunch at the Colbys' house, but that wasn't where they were. "Take us as you find us," Silvy had said the first time Jan had suggested this visit, and that was just what she'd have to do. The table, in the middle of the kitchen, looked pretty, though, with a yellow homespun cloth that Addie May's mother had woven for Ma and a jug of galax leaves in the center.

"Galax puts me in mind of funeral wreaths," Granny said. "They're the onliest plants I don't just fancy except for the cash they bring in."

At the Colbys', Silvy remembered, folks talked a good lot at mealtime, though not about funeral wreaths. Next thing Granny'd be telling about somebody fixing a spray of green corn with the ears left on for her Cousin Etta's funeral.

"Etta'd a-liked it fine, she bein' a great one for roastin' ears," was how Granny always wound up the story.

Silvy grabbed onto another subject fast, though maybe she didn't pick the best one in the world either.

"There's ramp," she said. "You don't care much for that either."

"There's some that fancies it in the spring," Granny said, "and, give it its due, it'll cure up a chest cold quick as scat." She cackled. "Cold goes somewheres else to git away from the smell of the ramp."

Jan looked puzzled.

"Ramp's a kind of wild leek," Silvy explained. "Real wild, like garlic and onion mixed, only worse."

" 'Tain't for the weak," Granny said, "it being so strong."

She looked around, sharp-eyed, to make sure everybody caught on to her little joke. Silvy had to give her credit for trying to be sociable, talking away when most times she tended strictly to her food like the rest of the family. Ma had put herself out some, too, with the tablecloth and the galax bouquet and dumplings to go with the ham, which, Silvy knew, was near about the last left in the smokehouse. Even Pa had been gabbier than common this morning, he being about as talkative as an old tree stump with strangers. It showed he meant well, but also it showed up the difference between him and Jan's father. Silvy couldn't imagine him shooting mistletoe off a tree or going bear-hunting either, any more than she could picture Pa cooped up in a bank, being looked at and talked to all day long.

"That was just delicious," said Jan, refusing a third helping of Ma's apple cobbler.

Jan's mother had taught her nice manners, but that was no sign of what she'd be saying at school next week. "Quaint" would be the best word she could come up with to describe her visit to the poor mountain people, and "backward" would be more likely. Let her talk then. Silvy advised herself to simmer down—no sense in getting all ruffled up about something she'd made up strictly out of her head, like picking a fight with her own shadow.

"Is your assembly program coming along all right?" Jan asked.

"Fine, just fine." There was no call for Jan to scare her that way, as though her program was going to be next week instead of away off in March sometime. "I'm working on it."

Working on it by thinking every so often that she didn't have a notion in her head about what to have that wouldn't sound backwoodsy. It wasn't so easy trying to jump back and forth between the town and the mountains, like one of those yoyos the kids used to play with, here, there, and back again.

"Juny's down yonder waiting on the mistletoe." Addie May stuck her head in the door. "Hi, Jan."

Addie May wasn't scared of anybody or impressed by them either, which was the right way to be, except that Silvy had wishy-washy spells.

"No need you girls coming back up the hill," Ma said. "I'll let you off the dishes. Water's not near to boiling anyway, and Kel'll be stopping by for you."

At the Colbys' the dishwasher would take care of the dirty plates, though even there the invisible Daisy would have to scrape the scraps off the dishes. Here, folks cleaned the last bite off their own plates with a chunk of corn pone, victuals not being all that easy to come by.

"Eat it up, every bite," Granny used to say when Silvy was little, "or you'll live to wish you had it back on your plate again."

Silvy looked doubtfully at the pile of mistletoe, which seemed to have swelled up just during dinner.

"Amongst us we can handle it easy," said Addie May, piling a big batch of it in Jan's arms.

Jan likely hadn't come expecting to be used as a pack mule, but she'd just have to take the bitter with the sweet —if there'd been any sweet so far, aside from the cobbler. The mistletoe didn't weigh so much. It just sprangled out so Silvy and Addie May and Jan looked like walking bushes as they stumbled down the lane to the music of "Higgledy Pop" from Jan's transistor.

The galax was already piled up in a corner of the cabin, along with the red and yellow bittersweet. Next month Pa would cut some Christmas trees to sell or let folks chop their own, and that'd be close to the last of the cash money until spring, aside from odds and ends of honey and preserves and maybe fresh pork that they'd set out of a sunny Sunday when folks might be riding around, grateful for their car heaters.

Cousin Juny already had his truck part full of mountain apples, some of Addie May's ma's handwoven wool scarves for the Craft Shop in town, and a few bushels of red and purple ears of corn that the flower man liked for winter table fixings.

"I'll see he doesn't shortchange you." Addie May climbed into the cab and rolled an eye in Jan's direction. "Got to watch these city slickers. Silvy, d'you want anything in town?"

There were plenty of things she wanted besides just wanting to go along, but paying for them was something else.

"I thank you, but I've near about got my shopping all done for this week."

Addie May grinned.

"How about that suede coat you were looking at—the one with the mink collar?"

"I decided against it," Silvy said.

She and Addie May had fun with this kind of fooling, but it wasn't the way to talk in front of Jan, who might think they were needling her—the little rich girl among the peasants. Addie May probably was doing just that, and Silvy had gone along with her, which she wished she hadn't. Jan hadn't said a single thing to make Silvy feel awkward on her visit to the Colbys', and Silvy wouldn't want it said that she hadn't returned the favor.

"Have a nice day," Silvy said, "and thank you for seeing to the mistletoe."

"You're surely welcome," said Addie May, always quick to pick up a message. "See you again, Jan."

Jan stood looking after the truck as it rattled down the road.

"You have fun around here," she said.

"Berries from the farthest-off bush always taste the sweetest," Granny sometimes said—which was maybe why Jan thought riding into town to peddle mistletoe was so great.

Silvy had been plenty fired up herself about her visit with Jan because it was so completely different from home. She couldn't truthfully say, though, that they had actually done anything very exciting. Just looking around had been enough for Silvy, though a person couldn't make a career out of just that.

"Miss?" A town-type man with a narrow, buttoned-up face and wary eyes stepped out of a car at the foot of the lane. "I'm looking for Mr. Kershaw."

"Gone bear-hunting," said Silvy. "Anything I can tell him?"

"I heard he might have some land for sale."

Silvy was about to say he'd heard mighty wrong because she was sure Pa wouldn't sell even one square inch of his ground.

"Ain't goin' to have people closin' in on me," he'd said plenty of times. "A man's got to have breathin' room."

Still, if this man could persuade Pa some way, it might help Silvy get away to college.

"Or I might be interested in a lease," the man went on. "That means I'd rent it for a period of years."

"Does it, now?" Did this slick character think Silvy was ignorant just because she lived back here in the cove? "He'll be back tomorrow or maybe the next day."

Or whenever the hunters got enough bear to satisfy them.

"If you'll tell him I called, he could telephone me at—"

"We don't have a phone," said Silvy.

"I'll stop by again then," he said, smooth as grease, "and thank you for the information."

"You're welcome," said Silvy, and away he went, down the road toward Clate's without even saying who to tell Pa had been there.

"I wonder who that was," said Jan, frowning. "I think I've seen him around town, but—"

"If he wants to see Pa real bad, he'll be back," said Silvy, "though he might as well save his breath and his gasoline. Now, where's Kel?"

Mostly it was Silvy that kept Kel waiting instead of the other way around. More than likely he'd found a batch of rocks somewhere and forgotten all about Silvy and Jan. He came in a minute, though, driving Clate's truck.

"Ready?" He bobbed his head in Jan's direction. "How're you?"

"Oh, fine. Do I get to ride in the truck?"

"Unless you want to walk nine miles."

"As it is, you won't have to walk but three, mostly straight up," Silvy put in.

"Climb in." Kel noticed the transistor, beating out "Blowing My Mind, Breaking My Heart." "Best if you leave that home."

Jan gave him a stubborn look.

"Why? The Dusty Answers are going to be on."

"How're you going to hang onto a radio and climb up the side of a hill?"

The truth was, Kel probably couldn't concentrate on minerals with people singing at the top of their voices about how up tight they were.

"We've got nervous-type rocks around here," Silvy said. "Can't sneak up on 'em if they hear us coming."

"Even if we play strictly rock music, heh, heh?" Jan said, but she laid the radio on the seat of her little car, which was pulled up beside the cabin to save jolting up the lane to the house.

It did seem to Silvy that Kel went out of his way today to prospect in the highest-up mine dumps, where the girls had to scramble to follow him. Jan puffed behind, saying hardly a word. Probably she needed all her breath for clambering up junior-grade cliffs and over gullies and ravines.

"Now, Kel," Silvy said finally, "Jan's beat out."

"I'm not," Jan said through her teeth. "You don't hear me complaining, do you?"

Not out loud, but Silvy was sure it would be a mighty long while before Jan let herself be dragged all over the landscape like this again. Besides, they didn't find anything that she and Kel hadn't found some of already—more samples of allanite, samarskite, and aquamarine, when she knew he had his mind set on something rare and wonderful, though he hadn't seen fit to tell Silvy what it was. Since that first time, he hadn't even mentioned about getting rich—which couldn't have been anything but just a daydream anyway. Sometimes when Silvy was worn out from poking through a bunch of rocks like a pig rooting for acorns, she almost got her courage up to speak her mind.

"It isn't fair," she'd say. "I'm plenty good to help you do whatever you're doing but not good enough to be told what it's supposed to be."

What held her back was that at least Kel was letting her share his subject for Appalachian Studies so she'd get her diploma if she never got a step farther. Chances were he'd have done just fine without her, or even better, except that with her along, they could look at twice as many rocks as if they were alone.

"I'll have to take the truck back to Clate's," he said when he finally decided they'd looked enough. "We can walk home from there." He glanced at Jan. "It's downhill all the way."

Maybe it'd be better for him to drop her and Silvy off at home and cancel out the visit to Clate's, but Silvy couldn't think of any other way to fill in the time. By the end of this day Jan wouldn't be in a mood to notice whether she was sleeping on an innerspring mattress like she was used to or on one of the feather beds Granny had brought along when she came to stay with Pa and Ma.

"This's Jan Colby," Silvy told Clate. "She'd like to see some of your gemstones."

Maybe Jan would and maybe she wouldn't. She looked mighty nigh as droopy as Silvy used to at the end of those first trips with Kel. A person got toughened up, but it took a while.

"Show her around, Silvy," Clate said. "You know where everything is."

"Pretty!" said Jan. "Beautiful!" but she said it standing on one foot and slipping her loafer off the other.

"Sit," said Silvy, "and I'll bring the things to you."

Bracelets, necklaces, and earrings from Clate's own designs, a tray of tumbled stones, a few faceted ones—Silvy showed them off to Jan, though her ears were practically flapping as she tried to listen to Clate at the same time.

"That fellow came back," Clate told Kel, "the one that was so almighty interested in your collection."

"What fellow?" Silvy asked.

"The one we met coming down the lane here that rainy day," Kel said vaguely.

"The one that was following us the other time!"

"The one you thought might maybe be following us the other time." He turned to Clate. "What'd he want?"

"Talking land, same as the first time. I told him I didn't know who he'd buy it from, not around here. Nice fellow, too—rock hound, I'd say. Asked some sensible questions about your minerals, anyway."

"Must be a land boom on," said Silvy. "A man stopped by our place right today, asking for Pa."

That one wouldn't care a nickel for rocks, though, Silvy knew just from looking at him for a few minutes.

"Thank you for letting me see." Jan, with both shoes on, remembered to make her manners to Clate as they left. "My mother has an idea for a pin that she's been wanting somebody to make up for her, so if she could come out—"

"Glad to talk to her." Clate hauled himself to his feet. "I'm here all the time."

Jan set her feet down careful as a basket of eggs as she and Kel and Silvy walked down the road toward home.

"Granny'll fix you something to soak your feet in," Silvy promised. "Could be you've got a blister."

"Could be I have," said Jan.

Silvy felt a pang of guilt. She should have remembered and so should Kel that in town people mostly didn't walk around much, so no wonder Jan had blistered feet.

"I'm real sorry," Silvy began.

"For what?" Jan still had some spunk left, blisters or no blisters. "It's all so—so different."

That was for certain sure. Day and night, sugar and salt, fire and water—Jan's life and Silvy's couldn't be any farther apart. Jan gave a gasp as they finally turned in at Silvy's lane.

"Why, what— But I'm sure I turned it off," she said.

From the seat of her car the transistor was giving its all to "Walking a Weary Road."

A middle-aged black car with two men in it moseyed past, then stopped and backed up.

"We're looking for Lud Bickett," one of them called.

In their faded denims and beat-up caps, they weren't town folks, but they didn't look right for mountaineers either. Silvy and Kel exchanged wooden glances. Anybody that looked like these two and were hunting Lud would just about have to be revenuers. Silvy found her voice first.

"Aren't any of us him. He lives back the way you came," she said, pointing.

Not that revenuers would probably knock on the door and ask where the blockaders were. They'd go skulking around through the woods, looking and sniffing, until they found what they were after along a creek somewhere. It was late in the season for blockading anyway, with hardly a leaf left on the trees to hide a still from the sharp-eyed government men.

"We heard he had a girl lives down this way," one of the revenuers said.

Silvy flushed.

" 'Twouldn't be anybody I know," she said.

If Lud had been going around saying she was his girl so even the revenuers had heard, Silvy didn't know but she'd turn him in herself if she knew where he was.

"It isn't so, anyway," she said out loud instead of just thinking it.

The government man grinned.

"No offense, miss." Jan's transistor, which she had retrieved from her car, was unfortunately playing "Pigs Are Looking for Me," but at a horrified glance from Silvy she turned it off. "If you see him around, ask him to stop by my office in town. Tell him Bob Sexton. He'll know."

"Yes, sir."

Silvy could just imagine Lud walking into the revenuers' office to be stuck in jail like a bear looking for a trap to be caught in. The more she thought about it, the more the car and its occupants reminded her of the ones that had followed Lud down the mountain before the football game —maybe to try and see what he had left off at his cousin's.

"We'll see him on the school bus Monday," Kel said, "and pass him the word."

"I thank you," the government man said, and drove off slow and easy as though he and his partner had all day today and most of tomorrow.

"They gone?"

Silvy jumped as Lud stuck his head up from where he was squinched down behind a boulder at the edge of the trees.

"Don't you be hanging around our place expecting us to keep the revenuers off you!" Silvy felt like slapping his face, even though he was twice as big as she was. "If you got trouble, take it on home with you."

"I ain't done nothin'," Lud said. "These fellers come up to the door askin' Ma where I'm at—"

"They did?" said Silvy, astonished.

"They did! But I heard 'em and lit out cross-country. I was lookin' for Addie May anyhow."

"Pity you wouldn't look for her where she lives, and anyway she's gone to town."

"If you're thinkin' I'm blockadin'," Lud said, "I ain't." That was no sign his relatives weren't, though. "That's out of style. I keep tellin' Pa that pot's what a feller ought to—" Seeming suddenly to remember that Jan was there, he hastily dropped that subject. "I just might go and see what this Sexton wants—on the thirty-second of February some year."

"Was it you that left Jan's transistor playing?" Silvy asked.

"Yeah. Seen that car a-comin' and hightailed it outa there." He turned to Jan. "Sorry about that."

"And that was what you might call the highlight of the weekend," Silvy told Addie May on the bus Monday. "I was never so humiliated in my entire life."

Jan, going home right after noon dinner Sunday on account of homework, had told Silvy three times and Ma twice what a good time she had had, which likely she'd have said even if the roof had blown off and the well gone dry.

"It was fabulous, just fabulous," she had said—which was carrying manners a little far.

"Hurry back," Silvy had said, not to be outdone, and Jan had gone, with the transistor going loud and clear with "I Never, No, Never Said Love Was Forever."

Silvy liked music her own self, but not every minute of

the day. It was hard to think with all that racket, and thinking was what Silvy had better be doing a lot more of. Mostly she ought to think about next year, though if she did decide on something, she didn't see how she'd manage to do it unless she and Kel discovered some absolutely fantastic minerals somewhere.

"Anyway, it's over and done with." Silvy and Addie May climbed down from the bus in the school parking lot. "She's come and gone and knows the worst."

And Silvy didn't owe her anything any more, which was a big load off her mind. The funny thing was, Silvy felt sorry for Jan, in a way. She just didn't seem to get very fired up about anything unless maybe radio music. If Silvy was in her shoes— But how did Silvy know how she'd feel about things if she were Jan, who took for granted things that Silvy worked her head off for and then mostly didn't get?

"What I have to do is think up something for this program," Silvy said mournfully. "I've got some time on it yet but not the first idea what to have."

"I'd favor something that fits in with us being like we are," said Addie May. "If we're important enough so we're spending a whole year studying ourselves, seems we should be able to get us up one piddling little ol' program."

"Seems we should, only—"

It wouldn't be practical for Pa to shoot down either mistletoe or a bear in the school auditorium or for Addie May's ma to set up her loom and weave some cloth or for Lud to strangle that famous bobcat all over again. Pa and Ma could sing real pretty with the dulcimer, but they'd never in the world do it in front of the whole school.

In a way, Silvy thought Addie May was right about the program having something to do with life in the coves and hollows, but in another way she didn't. Why get up something about the old ways when pushing out into the mainstream of life was what to do, according to the TV? Besides, what did the kids at school care about how folks did back in the mountains? It was a problem, sure enough.

"I'll ask Kel," Silvy decided, though unless he could set up a program based entirely on rocks, he'd be about as much help as a flea at a dog fight.

Pa, with Bugle, Bet, and old Blue tagging at his heels, came back from the bear hunt that evening around first dark, tired, dirty, and loaded with bear meat. He hollered Ma and Silvy down to the road to give him a hand with his gear.

"Got us two pretty good bear." He rummaged in his jacket pocket and brought out a few bills that he passed over to Ma. "Nothing would do but I had to sell mine's hide to Doc. Seems he always wanted a bearskin rug. Head, teeth, and all, he's figgerin' on." He grinned at Ma. "D'you call to mind that time at your pa's I got bit in the leg by a bear rug, trippin' over it in the dark?"

"I do," said Ma. "A wonder Pa didn't have to carry that rug to the tooth-dentist, chewing on tough meat thataway."

Hearing Pa and Ma joking about something that had happened long before Silvy was born gave her a nice, steady feeling of being linked to a whole chain of people going back just about forever. Ma's grandpap had come to the mountains from the coast to get clear of too many close-in neighbors, and before that a whole batch of folks had crossed over the water from the highlands of Scotland. Pa and Ma might be about fifty years behind the times and just barely scratching out a living, but they—and Silvy, too—had their roots planted firm as rock in the hills. Silvy hated to be the one to break away, like snapping off a stem of something and trying to make it grow somewhere else in a different kind of soil, but if it grew better—

Ma put the money in her pocket without looking at it,

but Silvy decided it must be anyway twenty dollars. It just went to show that money came from mighty unexpected places sometimes. Other times it didn't come from the expected ones, like the time Ma made a quilt to order for a woman up the country and she never did come back to fetch it away. Pa dug around in his jacket pocket some more and pulled out a booklet.

"Doc sent this for you," he told Silvy in a puzzled voice. "I didn't just get the straight of it, but it seems some teacher of yourn asked Mrs. Doc for the loan of it for you, so seeing Doc was going to see me—"

Highcliff College—Silvy stared at the lettering on the cover.

"I told Doc his missus had likely mistook the message; you weren't planning on any more schooling noways."

How did Pa know what Silvy was planning, though wanting would be a better word? He had never asked, and Silvy had never offered. What would be the use? Pa didn't have the wherewithal to help, even if he was of a mind to. The army had grabbed Bobby right out of high school, and Arvilla hadn't even finished, so why would Pa ever imagine that Silvy, the least one of all, might have different notions? Silvy ruffled the leaves of the booklet.

"No harm just thinking," she said.

No harm but no good either, Silvy being situated the way she was. Pa, trudging up the lane laden down like a mule, looked worn out all of a sudden.

"I can take some more of that gear off you," Silvy offered.

"No need. My back ain't broke yet."

He didn't say another word until he'd put the bear meat to hang in the corncrib, where it'd keep good and cold and not stir up too much interest from the dogs. Ma, who hadn't said anything either, hung the blanket on the rail fence to air and took the battered coffeepot inside to wash it. Pa came back out of the corncrib and sat down on a big old stump to clean his rifle.

"Silvy!" he said, sober-faced. "Tell me this. Whatever do you want to go for, way over yanside of the mountain?"

"See what's there, I guess," Silvy mumbled.

"High-priced looking, for poor folks." Pa sighted down the rifle barrel.

"This's only a little bitty piece of the world," said Silvy. "There's lots of things to see out yonder."

"Nobody's going to cover it all," he said. "Might as well be satisfied with where you're at."

"Were your folks way back satisfied with where they were at?" Silvy demanded. "Couldn't rest until they got somewhere else, clear across the water."

"You kin look at TV and see more'n you could travel to in a lifetime."

"I'm not aiming to travel every place there is. I just want to learn things."

She didn't know why she was wasting her breath this way, likely making Pa feel bad because he couldn't help her do what she wanted. A new thought struck him.

"You won't take charity to go, Silverbell. That I won't hear of."

Pa and his precious pride! Silvy hadn't expected any different—hadn't expected even to let Pa know her wishes. For a long time she hadn't been over sure about wanting to go, but talking about it now made her absolutely certain. She didn't know that even college was the answer to everything, but anyway it'd be a step in some direction, better than staying rooted to the spot forever. She sighed.

"Wantin' and gettin'," she said, "are two different things."

"That's what I hear." Pa got out his oily wiping rag and

worked it down the inside of the rifle barrel. "No use talking. I can't handle it noway. I could easier fly to the moon."

"Folks do," said Silvy, "but not on their own money." She looked at his sober face. "No need for you to fret. 'Can't' is a word it's hard to get around." She skipped briskly away from the subject. "A man stopped by to see you."

"Yeah? Say what he wanted?"

Silvy decided that was something best left alone.

"Said he'd be back."

Pa started to put the gun back together again.

"Tell your ma I'll eat soon's I finish this."

Silvy took her Highcliff booklet up to her room under the rafters and laid it on the chest. She could read it tonight just for pure entertainment, the same as the story books from the library. It was a relief some ways to have the college business out in the open and know for certain sure she couldn't expect any help from Pa. She had known it all the time, of course, but still she had held a small, foolish dream in the back of her head that had about as much substance to it as the cobwebs that glittered in the field with the morning dew on them. Wish on a star, count a hundred white horses, knock on wood—nary a one did a speck of good, but a person had to halfway believe, just in case.

Frowning, Silvy moved some of her gemstones around on their canvas bed. As soon as she got a few more pieces from Clate, she'd have her stone bouquet just about the way she wanted it and could glue it down, although why she was bothering she didn't know, except that it was pretty.

"So that's how it is," she told Addie May the next morning. "This Highcliff's got a work program, making things to sell in the craft shops or waiting tables or growing stuff for this hotel they've got. They'd be crazy for somebody that could quilt like Granny and Ma or weave like your ma or— Trouble is, most of us young'uns don't follow the old ways. Besides, no reason they'd let me come when there must be five hundred others just as anxious and a heap cleverer."

"You're real set on this," Addie May said.

Silvy was. She didn't know for sure why, either, except it looked like the only way out of a life style that sure as fate was about to wither and die. She loved the mountains for looks, but she didn't think being poor in a pretty place was all that much better than off in a grimy city somewhere.

"You might could get you a job this summer," Addie May said, "at the Drive-In. I got the promise of a place if I can get a ride in every day."

Silvy was pretty sure Pa would never hear of her getting dressed up in a short-skirted uniform and hauling trays to a lot of parked cars. She could maybe baby-sit some, but there again she'd have to have a way to get to town and back. Working for Clate would be the best of all, but he was like everybody else around here, scratching to make enough in the summer to carry him through the winter. The money he gave her and Kel for finding rocks wasn't piling up real fast and wasn't likely to, either.

"I'm between a rock and a hard place, for sure," Silvy said, "and likely to stay there."

"Did you get the information I sent about Highcliff?" the librarian asked when Silvy came in at noontime to look up some of the minerals Kel and Clate had been talking about the day Clate had given her the gemstones.

"Yes, ma'am, and I thank you," Silvy said.

"I'll be glad to help you fill out the application if you're still interested."

"Oh, I'm interested, all right." Knowing she wanted to go wasn't any great improvement over just wondering. "The thing is, I don't just see my way clear."

"Their work program might be useful," the librarian said, "especially if you're good in crafts."

"I'm not." There was no point telling lies when the truth would be bound to come out. "I could wait tables if they don't have too many doing that already."

"There's no harm trying. Come in tomorrow noon if you can, and we'll get started."

"Yes, ma'am."

The librarian—Mrs. Duncan, her name was, according to the sign on her desk, which Silvy hadn't checked on before—was bound and determined. She was riding for a mighty big fall, too, right along with Silvy. The difference was that Silvy was expecting it.

"She's wasting her time," Silvy told Kel as they burrowed through another mine dump part way up Barefoot Mountain the next Saturday. "I take it kindly of her, but—"

Highcliff was a mighty pretty place, according to the pictures in the catalog—nothing extra-fancy in the way of buildings, but plenty of big trees to make shade and some far-off mountains poking their heads up into the sky. Silvy could feel at home there, as far as scenery was concerned, though scenery wasn't the main object and feeling at home wasn't either. Some days, riding home on the bus, she could imagine herself hurrying along the walkways at Highcliff with an armload of books, studying in the library, and—

"I already put my bid in there," Kel said, "long ago."

"You did?" Mad as a hen in a rainstorm, Silvy gave him a scorching look. "And never gave a thought to me, after all the traipsing around I've done"—her voice broke—"chasing after your hateful old rocks!"

Kel laid his prospector's hammer carefully down on a rock, though from the looks of him he'd rather rap Silvy's knuckles with it.

"Hateful, huh? That's how much you care about rocks!"

"So all right. I can't help it if they don't turn me on, can I? I'm still studying them, just the same."

"And you said your own self you didn't know if you even wanted to go to college."

"That was then. Now I do."

"And tomorrow maybe you won't again."

"Yes, I will! My mind's made up. Doesn't matter anyway, does it? I won't get to go, either way."

"Won't if you don't try—that's for sure," Kel mumbled.

"How're *you* figuring on getting there?"

"Science scholarship. If I can come up with something special on rocks, I'll have anyway a chance." His face sobered. "Only thing is, I'm lacking some of the rocks I need."

"Those!" They'd be cyrtolite, clarkeite, pyrochlore, and some others he'd mentioned a mighty long time ago. Silvy had meant to read up on them, every one, but she hadn't gone far with it yet. "What're you planning to prove with them?"

"Not *planning* to prove anything," he said impatiently. "Just waiting for the rocks to have their say."

"And taking their own good time about saying it, too." That remark was pure meanness. She knew good and well what Kel meant. At least the gemstones were pretty to look at, especially if Silvy could get them arranged to suit her in her flower picture. "I thought you had it in mind to discover a mine."

"I won't deny I might have had some such notion," Kel said, "but there've been experts working on that for a hundred years, and likely they didn't miss much. Maybe, though, if I get a chance to study some more—"

His face was so bleak that, put out as she was, Silvy couldn't help feeling sorry for him. Maybe he wasn't so almighty certain about getting to college as he talked.

"If anybody gets to go, you will," she said.

She wasn't sure she believed that. Kel was only a poor mountain kid, same as Silvy, with nobody to help him but himself.

"Well, back to the rock pile." She started rooting through the dump again. "If you ask me, this's getting things the hard way—or not getting them, more likely."

"Don't do it, then!" Kel was as touchy as she was today. "I'll take you home any old time."

"Oh, no, you won't." Silvy'd just as lief go, especially with a little snow already fluttering out of a dark cloud over the mountains, but she'd never give Kel the satisfaction of saying she was a quitter. "You're not going to get rid of me thataway. I'll hang in here if it kills me."

Kel's lips twitched.

"It might not. Can't hardly count on anything any more."

"And not only that, Mr. Kelsey McLeod—"

Not only that, she'd study until she knew everything Kel did about his crazy rocks. Then some fine day when he was thinking how hen-headed little ol' Silvy was, she'd say, "Cyrtolite, of course, is—" or, "Some experts think that allanite may be—" Oh, my, wouldn't that be the day!

"Readily soluble in sulfuric acid," Silvy read from the rock book lying open in front of her on Clate Fowler's worktable. "Dilute acid with water one to six."

Silvy hummed cheerfully to herself. As far as she could see, these chemical tests for rocks weren't much different from cooking recipes, so much of this and so much of that. Kel wasn't much taken with the idea of her even trying to run any tests, though she couldn't see why.

"I can read as well as anybody," she had argued.

"Just don't do them unless I'm here. A lot of the acids can act up on you."

He had flatly refused to teach her how to use the blow-pipe.

"You'd set yourself afire," he had muttered.

All the same, she was planning to have a try at that, too, sometime when Kel wasn't around. Right now he was out in the back room with Clate, sorting through a lot of rocks that he and Silvy had collected and hadn't had a chance to look at until now, when the weather was too cold for them to go out hunting more.

Silvy took the sulfuric acid bottle down from the shelf over her head and carefully measured out some of the oily-looking liquid into a glass beaker. She figured rapidly in her head—one part acid to six parts water, a matter of simple arithmetic. She ran water into a measuring cup and dumped it into the acid and—whoosh! The mixture seethed and fumed and boiled over violently onto Clate's worktable. Silvy jumped back but not quite fast enough. She gave a yelp of pain as little spatters of acid burned her hand. Kel came pounding in from the back room. He took one look, pushed Silvy over to the faucet, and stuck her hand under the running water.

"Clate!" he yelled. "You got any baking soda?"

"In the kitchen. I'll fetch it." Clate hurriedly mixed up a paste of soda and water and plastered it on Silvy's hand. Sniffing, he glanced at the worktable. "Sulfuric acid? What were you trying to test out?"

"Uraninite," Silvy said. "The book said it'd dissolve in sulfuric acid and—" She looked at Kel's tight-lipped face. "How'd I know it'd do that way?"

"You knew I said don't fool around with this stuff unless I'm right here," Kel said. "You near about ate a hole in Clate's table. What'd you do—pour the water into the acid instead of the other way around?"

"Yes," Silvy said sulkily. "What difference'd that make? Mix two things together, they ought to act the same way every time, no matter which you put in first. If you're making corn bread, it doesn't matter do you dump the cornmeal into the water or the water into the cornmeal. It's unfair—that's what it is."

Besides, her hand hurt, baking soda or not.

"Nothing unfair about it," Kel said. "It's a law of chemistry. It makes all that steam because—"

"Oh, skip it!" Silvy snapped. "Sorry about your table, Clate. I'll get Pa to plane this'n down or fix you a new one."

"No need," Clate said mildly. "I can turn the top over and use it bottomside up."

"I'll go on along home now," Silvy said with dignity. "I wouldn't doubt Granny has some balm that'll take the sting out of my hand."

What Silvy needed worse was some kind of balm that'd heal the hurt to her pride, but even Granny wouldn't be able to manage that.

"I'll walk over with you," said Kel.

"Not necessary," Silvy said haughtily.

Did he think she couldn't get the little way between Clate's place and her own house without setting the woods on fire or spraining her ankle in a woodchuck hole? It was just when she messed around with Kel's sneaky chemicals that she ran into trouble. All the same, Kel stumped along beside her, looking as though he was fixing to boil over just like that sulfuric acid. So all right, let him boil. What made him think he was the onliest one that could do anything? It'd be a satisfaction to believe that even Kel had nigh blown himself up, too, when he was starting out, but she knew better. Kel would have studied what the books said and figured and pondered until he couldn't make even one mistake. It was mighty unsettling trying to keep up with somebody like that, and in a way Silvy wished she hadn't even tried. Pride was gnawing at her again, though, and she was bound and determined to show him she wasn't a complete dimwit.

"I thank you," Silvy said when he took her to the door, which he didn't usually do. He even stepped inside to tell Ma and Granny what the trouble was. Granny took Silvy's little hand in her gnarled old one.

"I got just the thing," she said. "Some of my goldenseal salve'll heal it so there won't be ary a mark. Never fails me."

"'Tisn't all that big of a hurt," Silvy said, putting up a big front for Kel's benefit. "A few little splitter-splatters of acid is all."

She got some sympathy off and on from Addie May and Lud going back and forth in the school bus, but Kel never mentioned the subject again, probably figuring what had happened was her own fault for doing what he said don't do.

"Know that Bob Sexton that was looking for me that day?" Lud asked one morning as the bus toiled over the icy road and blowing snow scudded across the pavement. "I went to see him."

"Here we go again!" Addie May sighed. "You never!"

"I did. Think I'm afeard of that crowd?"

"If you're so bold, how come you ran away when they were looking for you, then?" Silvy put in.

"Government men don't mean a fellow no good most times," Lud said, "but then I got thinkin'."

"I don't believe that, either," Addie May muttered to Silvy.

"They got nothin' on me, so what's to lose?" Lud went on.

"We're listenin'," Addie May said. "What did they want? You to turn informer, maybe?"

"They know better'n that." Lud paused for effect. "What they wanted, they wanted me to help set up a still for one of the exhibits along the parkway."

"If you're fibbin', might as well tell a real genuine

whopper," Addie May said. "The government wants you to set up a still? Along the parkway, where it's twice as illegal as it is anywhere else?"

Lud wagged his head.

"That's what the man said. Couldn't hardly believe it my own self—ain't sure I do yet. More'n likely it's a trap—con me into doing something or 'nother they can throw me in the jailhouse for. Pa said forget it; they're likely just trying to get me to let drop who makes blockade around here. Onliest one I know is Pa's Cousin Sam, and they got him locked up already and threw away the key."

Silvy, not much interested in Lud's tales, took a last look at the report she was going to give today for her and Kel's mineral project. Turn and turn about was how they did it, Silvy one week and Kel the next, telling what all they found and where.

Kel, sitting behind her, craned his neck, likely trying to read over her shoulder. Silvy slammed her notebook shut. Kel never seemed much taken with her reports, which leaned to the history of mining in the state or where the different minerals got their names, all things she could find in a book or government pamphlet. Kel was purely scientific himself, with a lot of talk about the shapes of crystals, which minerals occurred together, and the chemical tests he used to identify them. Silvy smiled to herself. Kel was due for a great big surprise this morning, not because she probably knew anything he didn't, but because she had finally gotten on the track of what he was doing. She laid her cheek against the cold glass of the window for a minute.

"You got a fever?" asked Addie May.

"Seems hot in here."

Truth to tell, now that she was about to talk about what she'd found out that Kel didn't know she had, she felt a little on the shaky side. She hadn't felt quite this way since the Christmas program in first grade when she had to say a piece about bells ringing and children singing. She turned her head just enough to catch a glimpse of Kel's expressionless face, like a door tight shut against anybody wanting to look in. Could be he'd open up a little when she made it clear that she could keep up with him and that, if he got a scholarship for rocks, she might be able to, too.

Her face clouded, thinking of Ma and Pa and Granny trying to help her out with her college plans. She couldn't rightly call them plans, though—just hopes, and slim ones at that. Silvy had never thought her folks would even try to help, but they had.

"I got some buryin' money put away," Granny had said. " 'Tisn't much, but you're welcome to it. I kin keep on breathin' a while longer if I got to."

Knowing how Granny had saved a few pennies today and a few more next week, Silvy felt the tears coming to her eyes.

"I thank you kindly," she said, "but you hang onto your money. I'll make do some way. If I don't get to go next year, the year after'll be just as good."

It wouldn't, though. Skip a year and she'd likely never ever get away. Most folks didn't, settling down to one way of life and never shaking themselves loose from it.

Then one night Silvy had heard Pa talking downstairs after she had gone up to bed.

"I been ponderin' on this," he told Ma. "Silvy's got her heart set on it, you figure?"

"Most of us 've had our hearts set on things a lot of times and never got 'em," Ma said. "Scarcely anybody ever died of it."

"I got by without no extra schoolin'—just readin', arithmetic, and a little writin'."

"You did," Ma said, "but times 've changed some."

"Never starved to death yit," Pa went on, "nor froze either. What more does a feller want?"

134

"You've done real good," Ma said, "but young folks is different nowadays. They're big wanters." She paused for a minute. "Maybe she's goin' to need to make her own way. She might not be lucky enough to catch her a man like you. They're gettin' real scarce here in the mountains."

"Kelsey McLeod's a good boy."

"He's set on more studyin', too, I hear," Ma said. "Think he's ever goin' to come back here to get our Silvy once he's out in the wide world and her a mile behind him in what she knows?"

Pa sighed.

"I'll go down to the feldspar plant and see kin they use an extra hand," he said in an angry voice. "Cooped up breathin' all that dust! I'd just as lief be shut up in a cave somewheres, but I kin stand it a while."

Silvy had a notion to yell down through the knothole in the floor and tell him don't do it if it hurt him so bad, but it turned out there wasn't any need. The feldspar plant wasn't hiring just then.

"Have to take up blockadin', I reckon," Pa grumbled. "Till I get caught. You kin come see your pa in the jailhouse."

"Don't you dare do any such of a thing," Silvy said— not that he likely ever would. "If I can't get there legal, I won't go."

"Maybe you wouldn't a-liked the place anyway," Pa said.

"Maybe I wouldn't," Silvy agreed.

Pa brightened.

"Water not fit to drink, time they've ruint it with all their chemicals. Air full of smoke so you can't take a deep breath. Hard ol' pavement to walk on—"

"Instead of rocks and mud like we got here," said Silvy, a little sharp in the tongue.

Pa had been good to try to help, but he wasn't feeling

real brokenhearted about not being able to. What it all boiled down to was that whatever Silvy got, she'd have to get for herself—which was no news to her. Whether she was going about it the right way, sticking with Kel and his minerals, was something she wasn't sure about. She didn't have anything to lose, though—no way to go but up. More than likely, she'd stay right where she was, tied to the mountains forever.

"We're here." Addie May tugged at her sleeve. "Are you so scared of giving your report that you're planning to hide in the bus all day?"

"No, no!"

Silvy jumped up and rushed out of the bus. She was downright nervous by now, not because of standing up to give her report, which she'd done several times already, but because Kel might spot some mistakes in what she had to say. She had checked everything over a dozen times, but that was no sign that what she had read was every word true.

"Silvy." Miss Henderson called her name. "Your turn."

"Yes, ma'am." Silvy's voice shook a little as she stood up behind Miss Henderson's desk, the way everybody always did for their reports. She flipped frantically through the pages of her report, page 1 having hidden behind page 5 out of pure meanness. "In our study of the minerals of this area, which include gemstones and the fairly common feldspar and mica, which are mined commercially, we are specializing in a study of minerals which contain the so-called rare earth metals."

She paused to see, without looking straight at him, how Kel was taking that. His eyebrows lifted slightly, but his face had its buttoned-up look again, blank as a sheet of paper with nary a word written on it. She didn't know just what she had expected—maybe for him to jump up yelling, "How'd you find that out?" or, "Hey! That's classified information!" like in the spy stories she watched on TV. Silvy read steadily on, with never another look in Kel's direction.

"They're not earths and they're not overly rare, because more than two hundred minerals contain the rare earth elements, which are a group of fifteen metals." Silvy glibly reeled off the list: thulium, cerium that Clate used to polish his rocks with, promethium, samarium, yttrium, and the rest. "Local minerals that contain rare earths are samarskite, columbite, euxenite, monazite, allanite, pyrochlore, clarkeite, uraninite, and cyrtolite, some of which we—Kel and I—haven't been able to find."

Oh, she did sound learned, and she hoped Kel was impressed. She took a deep breath and turned to the next page.

"The rare earths have a large number of uses." If Kel thought she had stopped with just the names of things, he could guess again. "Misch metal, a mixture of rare earth metals, is used as an alloy with copper, nickel, aluminum, and magnesium. Rare earths are also used in an alloy for lighter flints, in carbon-arc-electrode cores for high-speed photography, in the glass industry, in color TV tubes, magnets, and paint dryers. Most interestingly, they are used in rods inserted in atomic reactors to regulate the rate of fission."

Silvy finished up just before the bell rang for the end of class.

"Congratulations!" Kel said in a deadpan voice as they all filed down to the cafeteria with their lunch bags.

"You knew it all already," Silvy said, "even if I didn't."

"One thing I didn't know."

"Only one? What was that?"

"I didn't know you could figure all that out your own self."

"You needn't be so surprised," Silvy flared. "I've got

brains, haven't I? Besides, it's all written down in the library if you look enough places."

"Took some organizing, anyway, and a lot of research. Wouldn't have hurt for you to discuss it with me ahead of time, though, so's not to double up on our work. We're supposed to be doing this together."

"Discuss it?" Silvy thumped her lunch basket down on the nearest table. "When did you ever discuss anything with me except to say, 'This here's what we're looking for.' You made a great big mystery out of the whole thing and never once told me the why and wherefore—just expected me to tag along like a"—her voice quavered —"like a little ol' puppy dog. Onliest difference was you never threw me even one bone."

"Saddest story ever I heard." Kel picked up her lunch and transferred it to a table for two. "If we're going to fight some more, might as well do it in private."

"I'm not going to fight. I've already had my say."

"I haven't had mine. First off, what'd be the sense of loading your brain down with something you don't care a nickel about? You said your own self that rocks don't turn you on—just a way to get your diploma."

"And a scholarship, too, don't forget."

"What you'd get it for would be to study mineralogy, and I don't figure you could make-believe on that for four long years." He took a big bite out of his ham-and-biscuit sandwich. "Second, you're burning to get out of here, no matter how. Me, too, but I'm aiming to come back."

"Come back? Whatever for?"

"Well, I—" He looked as though he wished he hadn't ever gotten into this discussion. "You get something, you got to pay back however you can, so I figure if I get me an education out of the minerals and all, I'd kind of feel beholden."

Silvy put down her corn bread and stared at him.

"Beholden to a bunch of rocks?"

"Not the rocks exactly—the place they come from." He abandoned the subject. "Eat up. We got to get back to class."

"I'm not hungry."

She sat there churning what he had said around and around in her head. In a way she understood what he meant—being beholden was something she didn't much fancy herself—but it did seem impractical.

"What you aiming to do for the place?" Granny had said long ago that Kel was a thoughty one, but this time and plenty of other times he was too deep for Silvy. "Doesn't look to me like those mountains need any help from you."

"This place isn't just the mountains; it's the folks that live here, too," Kel said as though that ought to be as plain as day. "When I get some more learning, I could maybe figure out a better way to extract what rare earths we got in the ore around here and make some more jobs. Right now that branch of mining doesn't hardly pay except off somewhere." Trust Kel to know a lot of things that Silvy had never thought of. "Or I could work in the mineral museum for the Park Service, getting up exhibits to show folks what all we got in this area. I could—"

The bell clanged for the end of the lunch hour, and Kel gulped the last bite of his sandwich. Silvy jumped up, too, so fascinated by Kel's unusual notions that she never quite finished her lunch.

All the way home that afternoon she mulled over what he had said while Addie May and Lud jabbered on about the still that Lud said he had been asked to set up. One thing about Lud, he had plenty of imagination, hard to tell from plain ordinary lying sometimes.

Silvy might as well face up to the fact that everything Kel said was true. Those rare earths of his did leave her mighty cold. The onliest reason she had looked up all she had about them was to prove to Kel that she could find out what he was about and to see if she could get a scholarship, too. Now she had proved the one, but in case she did get the scholarship, she'd be honor bound to keep studying minerals, and that she just plain didn't want.

"You feeling all right?" Addie May wanted to know.

"I guess," Silvy said listlessly.

Seemed she couldn't make anything work right. She felt like a pig in quicksand—no way out and no rope handy. She and Addie May and Kel got down off the bus and fanned out, each in a different direction, without another word. Bugle and Bet and old Blue came tearing down the snowy lane to meet Silvy in case she had any lunch left. She did, a little smidgen of corn bread and a nibble of ham, more suitable for one lone chipmunk than for three sizable dogs.

"It's the thought that counts," Silvy said, doling out crumbs. Even dogs didn't get the breaks some days.

Pa was whacking away at something in his shop—another chair maybe—and Ma and Granny were bent over the quilting frame in the kitchen.

"We got us a new pattern," Granny said cheerfully.

"Pretty." Silvy dutifully admired squares of white and pale pink set together with strips of springtime green.

"This here's called Silverbell," Granny said. "Kind of brightens up a winter day."

It would take more than that to brighten up this day. Silvy went up to her own little room and set down her books. On her study table the flower picture she had made out of the stones Clate had given her shone in the last of the light. She looked with satisfaction at the design of flowers and leaves that she had finally glued onto their canvas background before she went to school early this morning.

"Leave it lie flat until the glue sets good," Clate had said.

"There's more weight to a bunch of little stones than a person'd think."

Silvy looked admiringly at her creation. This was one thing that had turned out just right—a winter flower garden all her own. As soon as she made up her mind where she wanted to hang it, she'd get Pa to drive a nail in the wall, maybe opposite the window where the sun would shine on it of a morning and make the stones glitter. Yes, that'd be the best. She held the picture up to try how high it ought to be. Up a little—

"Oh!"

Her eyes widened as, like a winter avalanche, her beautiful stones began to slide slowly and then faster and faster. They clattered to the floor in a heap, leaving only a little tigereye bumblebee sticking stubbornly in place.

"What you could do," said Kel, lingering with Silvy at the end of the lane while Addie May's Cousin Juny turned the bus around and headed for home, "is make you a gem-stone picture of that hearts-bustin'-with-love bush you showed me that time." He gave her a laughing look. "Now that you've got the hang of letting the glue dry before you try to hang up the picture."

She'd never hear the end of that from Kel or Clate either. She should have kept her mouth strictly shut about how she'd been in such a rush to see how her picture was going to look that Clate's warning about the glue had dropped right out of her mind.

"Garnet would be the right color," Kel said, still talking

about hearts-bustin'-with-love, "and that red hematite."

"Yes, it would." Silvy looked curiously over at the man in the town topcoat who had climbed out of his car in front of the sales cabin where Pa was standing. "In case Clate has any."

"Mr. Kershaw?" the visitor said, polite as the preacher come to dinner.

"Yeah, I'm him, worse luck." Pa looked grumpy, the way he mostly did lately.

Silvy clutched Kel's arm.

"There he is back again," she muttered under her breath, "the one that came and wanted to buy some of Pa's land that time, only Pa wasn't home."

Pretending not to look, Silvy saw the stranger stick out his hand in Pa's direction.

"Monteagle's the name," he said. "I got a little proposition for you."

"Might as well save your breath, friend," Pa said. "Whatever it is, I ain't buyin'."

"Oh, I'm not selling anything." He had been a smooth talker the other time and he still was. "I'm buying if we can make a deal."

Pa seemed to notice Silvy and Kel in the lane for the first time.

"Best get up to the house, Silvy," he said. "Hit's too cold to be standing around. G'bye, Kelsey."

"Yessir."

Kel headed for home down the road, and Silvy scooted up the lane. She slammed the back door good and loud, hoping Pa could hear it down by the road.

"It'd be a pity to knock the house down, cold as it is," Ma said mildly, glancing up from the quilt frame. "We'd all catch our death of a chill."

"Forgot something, even so," Silvy muttered.

She put down her books and lunch basket and stepped

outside again, closing the door soft as a kitten's step. By dodging around back of the corncrib, she could sneak down among the trees to the big boulder behind the sales cabin, where she could hear every word as plain as day.

"Hillbilly Heaven, I'm going to call it," this Monteagle was saying. "I figure that'd go over big."

Silvy waited for the explosion. Hillbilly Heaven! Pa must be so insulted that he was struck dumb. To her surprise, he talked along as easy as running water.

"You goin' to have one of them Ferris wheels and like that? Dancing girls and shooting galleries?"

"Everything you can think of, friend. Somebody making moonshine, old women in sunbonnets weaving or knitting or whatever, tame bears, plenty of sideshows, something for everybody."

Silvy could hardly believe it. Was Pa actually thinking about selling off his land, maybe to pay for Silvy's schooling? That was about as noble as Pa could get, loving solitude the way he did.

"Lots of that rock music?" Pa went on.

"A whole rock festival was what I had in mind for in the summer," Monteagle said. "I'm figuring on some big name outfits—the Dismal Swamps or the Moaning Mushrooms. Why, we'd have the kids piling in here by the thousands." He paused. "If you didn't want to pull up stakes entirely, I could leave you a few acres for your buildings. Whatever it is you sell, business would boom for you."

"Reckon it would." Pa let the silence settle for a minute. "If you can meet my price—"

Silvy held her breath. She couldn't imagine Pa anywhere else than right here in this spot, and she didn't know that she wanted him to make such an almighty sacrifice just for her.

"Name your price then," Monteagle said, "and we'll talk it over."

Pa's voice hardened.

"One million dollars," he said, "and no dickering."

"Wha-at?"

"Cash."

"Now, look, you're fooling."

"No, I ain't. This here's my home place and my folks' from away back, and I ain't lettin' it get messed up with no Hillbilly Heaven, clutterin' up the scenery and insultin' the mountain folks with a pack of foolishness!"

"Insulting?" Monteagle said. "How're your neighbors going to take it when they find out you're turning down something that'd make them a lot of jobs? That's the problem around here, isn't it—no jobs?"

"There's others 've got land hereabouts," Pa said. "Buy offen them if you can git you a deal—no nevermind of mine."

Monteagle wasn't one to give up right away.

"This location's far and away the best."

"That's my idea exactly, and it's me that's got it."

"Just think it over a few days. You got a girl to educate, I see, and—"

"Thinkin' won't make ary a bit of difference," Pa said. "A feller can't go against how he feels—not and be his own man."

Monteagle finally seemed to recognize a stone wall when he met one head on.

"If that's how you feel—"

"That's it," Pa said. "No hard feelings. Just you're one kind of feller and I'm another."

Silvy skittered out from behind the boulder and ran for the house. Tears were trickling down her face, though she wasn't sure exactly what for. Partly it was disappointment at seeing the wherewithal for her schooling going glimmering like a wisp of fog. More than that, though, the tears were on account of Pa, who hadn't sold himself out the minute somebody waved some cash money in his face.

Foolish, stubborn, selfish—Silvy could think of a lot of easy labels people could put on him for turning down an offer for his land, but Pa, aggravating as he could be lots of times, wouldn't be Pa if he wasn't true to his own self, like whoever it was in the Shakespeare play Silvy had studied in school.

"Silvy!" His voice caught her before she made it to the back door. "Didn't I tell you to go up to the house?"

Feet dragging, Silvy ambled back to meet him.

"I went." She stared at the ground. "You never said don't come back."

"You're too sassy by far. People that listen where they ain't meant to don't never hear anything good."

"Might not," Silvy agreed, "but could be they'd hear something that'd stick by them a lifetime."

Words could be troublesome, not always exactly what a person had in mind, but Pa must have gotten the drift.

"Pshaw, now, Silvy, all a man can do is what his nature tells him." He strode on up the hill, with Silvy trotting beside him. "Maybe something'll turn up at the feldspar plant in the spring." That was his way of saying he was sorry he'd had to do Silvy out of her schooling by hanging onto his land. "Smells like your ma's got our rations about ready."

All Silvy could notice as she sniffed the cold air was the familiar smell of wood smoke from the stove, not what was cooking on it. This time of year, eating got skimpy, with no fresh provender from Granny's summer garden nor any wild berries for a change-off from a winter diet of corn pone, cured meat once in a while, and whatever Ma had managed to store away in the root cellar. Things improved some a couple of days before Christmas, though, when Pa got lucky and came trailing home with a big old wild turkey he'd shot out in the woods.

"Here's our Christmas dinner," he yelled, tickled as a kid with a new whistle. "Biggest gobbler ever I seen!"

"I do declare!" Granny cried. "Ain't that a beauty now?"

"I'm real proud," said Ma, already making plans. "Corn-bread stuffing, I'd say, and a couple of apples stuck in to take out the wild taste. Oh, my, don't I wish the chestnut trees hadn't all died on us! Chestnut stuffin's just downright luxurious. Then I been savin' the last punkin for a pie and—"

Silvy sighed. Christmas around here was never very gifty, not the least bit like what it was supposed to be everywhere else, according to the TV. Granny usually knit mittens for Arvilla's young'uns a couple of mountains over, and Ma sewed Silvy a dress out of goods she'd traded fresh eggs for at the general store down by Bear Creek. The TV people, carrying on about diamond watches and store-bought toys and fancy sweaters, would think the Kershaws had a pretty sorry-type Christmas, and likely Jan Colby would think the same. Silvy had near about stopped fretting about what Jan Colby might think, though. In the first place, she didn't have any way of knowing for sure what it was, and, second, everybody lived different and no law against it.

Jan came out once in a while, though never to stay the night again. One day she had brought her mother to Clate's to see about his making the brooch Jan had asked about that first time. On the way back home Mrs. Colby and Jan had stopped at the roadside cabin to get some sourwood honey like the jar Ma had sent her for a guest gift when Silvy went visiting.

"You must come and stay with us again," Mrs. Colby had told Silvy.

Besides that, she had asked Ma to make her a quilt in blue and sunshine yellow "to match up with the room I stayed in," Silvy told Ma, and had bought two of Pa's chairs, which she said would be perfect in the family room.

Silvy hadn't just fancied their buying all that stuff if

they'd done it because they figured the Kershaws were short of cash, which they sure enough were, though not much more than usual. On the other hand, Pa gave good value with his chairs.

"They'll last you your lifetime," he had said, "and your grandbabies', too."

Likely Mrs. Colby didn't care would they last a lifetime or not, as long as they looked the way she thought they ought to right now. They weren't French Provincial by a long shot, but neither was the family room where Silvy and Jan had done their studying. Silvy could remember every single detail of the place, fussed and bothered though she'd been a good share of the time she was there.

"See you at school," Jan had said, departing.

Silvy didn't see her very often except in the halls now and then. Jan hadn't had to hold program committee meetings because everybody did their programs on time—the general, the peace speaker, a pilot from one of the airlines, somebody's uncle that had gone on a safari to Africa. All Jan did was to OK the plans and remind the ones that had programs coming up. With March looming up all too clear on the calendar, Silvy didn't need reminding. What she did need was a program. Over the Christmas vacation she'd absolutely have to sit down and work it all out. Anyway, she hoped she could. She hadn't had much luck working anything else out except the uses of the rare earths.

The day after Pa brought home the turkey, Silvy woke up to a few flakes of snow starting to sift down through the trees, just enough to settle in the dents and hollows but not cover the top.

"A white Christmas, if we're lucky," Granny said, stirring the chopped-up pieces of pumpkin to make sure they didn't scorch.

"I was hoping for a visit from Arvilla and Lamar and the young'uns," Ma said, "but they'll never in the world make it in a snowstorm in their old wore-out car."

Even without a snowstorm they'd never make it. Last time Silvy had seen their car, it puffed and panted like a bad case of asthma.

"Come spring, could be somebody'll be goin' that can carry you to make her a visit," Pa said, "or might be I could coax our car into running that far."

That'd be the day! Pa's car might totter into town and back once in a blue moon, but going up and over a couple of mountains was something else again. Ma looked mighty sober the rest of the day, turkey or no turkey, and Silvy didn't blame her. Arvilla's kids were the onliest grandchildren Ma had and so far off that she scarcely ever got a look at them. Granny, shaking off the snow, which was coming down strong now, brought in some branches of evergreen to put up over the fireboard, with some leftover bittersweet stuck in for brightness.

"It's pretty out, anyways," she said. "Bushes have got their new white bonnets on."

Ma, working the lard into the piecrust dough, didn't say ary a word.

"I might get out the dulcimer," said Pa, not used to Ma acting contrarious.

"Christmas ain't till tomorrow," she said in a muffled voice. "I'm too busy right now."

"I'll work on my chairs then." Pa got up and opened the door from the kitchen into the workshop, letting in a flood of cold air. "Kitchen stove'll warm 'er up in no time."

"Put on some more wood then, Silvy," Ma said. "Cain't let your pa freeze to death." She managed a smile that looked shaky around the edges. "Not on Christmas, anyhow."

"Wait'll I git the hogs kilt and the meat cured, why don't you?" Pa said. " 'Twouldn't be right to leave you a pore widow-woman with nary a bite to eat in the house." He cocked an ear toward the back door. "You hear something out there?"

He threw open the door. A voice, muffled by the snow, came faintly from down the lane.

"Come get us!" Pa dashed out as the voice came closer. "We're near-about froze!"

"Arvilla!" Ma ran out, too, to snatch the least young'un out of Arvilla's arms and to shoo the other snowy figures inside. "However did you get here?"

"Mighty nigh didn't." Arvilla tossed back her coat. "Lamar's cousin and his wife carried us to the crossroads— far as he could get on our road—and we walked on in."

"Where's Lamar at, then?"

"Pumpin' gas." Arvilla's face clouded. "The man couldn't get ary a soul to tend the pumps over Christmas, so Lamar said he'd oblige." Silvy knew what that meant. Lamar'd oblige because he needed the money bad, a fact that Arvilla was naturally too proud to admit. "Said seein' he'd be settin' in the gas station the whole time, I might as well have my Christmas here with you. Cousin George and them'll pick me up tomorrow after dinner if the road's clear, so we'll have to do our visiting real fast."

Ma started unwinding the children—Sal, Johnny, and little Noah—out of their worn wraps.

"Grown a mile!" she exclaimed. "Wouldn't hardly a-known any of you, you're so big! Let's see now. What've we got for a bite? Not much right now, but tomorrow, oh, my! We've got the biggest, fattest old turkey ever you saw!" The children looked at her round-eyed while she passed out cold corn pone spread with honey. "And I got a little milk left. How'll that do you?"

"Thought you'd be long gone from here by now," Arvilla said up in the room she and Silvy used to share and would tonight, too. The children would be strewn around on pallets on the floor, all but the baby, who'd sleep in with Granny. Right now Ma and Granny were working on the turkey and the pies while Pa let the young'uns play with wood scraps in his shop.

"Getting away's a heap easier said than done," Silvy said sharply. "I got to finish my schooling first."

She didn't have the heart to tell Arvilla that she had her mind set on going to college, too—not when it was plain that Arvilla and Lamar were having to scratch gravel just to keep eating.

"That's real pretty." Arvilla took an admiring look at the gemstone picture that Silvy had finally finished, with every stone set good and solid this time. "Puts me in mind of the mountain when the spring flowers are out."

"It's yours," Silvy said impulsively, "for a Christmas present."

She wasn't exactly a cheerful giver—goodness knew when she'd ever get any more rocks to make another picture for herself—but poor Arvilla had mighty near nothing that was just purely for prettiness.

"I wouldn't want to rob you," said Arvilla, but her eyes shone with pleasure.

"No robbery. I can make me another."

"You can? Now, aren't you the clever one!"

Not clever enough to get what she wanted, though she wasn't going to give up just yet. Seeing Arvilla so worn-looking made Silvy more determined than ever not to wind up walking the same weary road. It shamed her to use her own sister for a horrible example, and likely Arvilla wouldn't look at herself quite that way, though she'd said often enough, well out of Lamar's hearing, not to do what she'd done.

Anyway, there were presents for the children on Christmas morning—new warm mittens all around, one of Granny's cornhusk dolls for Sal, and flipperdingers that Pa had made for the little boys.

"Blow on it, Johnny!" Pa said. "No, no, thisaway!" The

flipperdinger looked a good bit like an Indian peace pipe, except it had an acorn cup cemented to the stem instead of a pipe bowl. Inside the cup was a little pith ball. "See, I got it!" When Pa blew—not too much, not too little, like Kel with the blowpipe—the ball rose above the cup on a stream of air. Pa grinned at the boys' astonishment. "One of these times I'll make you a gee-haw-whimmy-diddle, too."

"You could make some for the shop," Silvy said. "The tourist kids'd go wild over them."

"Could," said Pa, which meant maybe he would and maybe he wouldn't.

Pa was real notiony about what he made. The mood had to strike him before he'd ever begin, but at least Silvy, who couldn't help herself over much, was trying to help Pa with a new idea.

Ma had been up since before day to stick the turkey into the oven, where it'd get good and tender with long cooking.

"Did I know how many years it's been sashayin' through those woods, it'd be a help," she said. "A turkey don't get that big overnight."

Everybody but Pa, who was working on a dulcimer, for a wonder, stayed close to the stove all morning so as not to miss out on any of the wonderful smells that filled the kitchen.

"Clackety-clack!" Pa called from the shed. "Ain't heard so much talk since the last quiltin' bee."

"Hear away," said Ma. "The quiet'll settle soon enough. You can come and set. Everything's ready."

Crackling brown turkey, fluffy potatoes that Granny had whipped to a froth, ruby-red beets from the root cellar, pumpkin pies spicy with nutmeg—Silvy couldn't remember such a dinner, not even the one she'd eaten at the Colbys'.

"I want you to carry the bulk of this turkey home with you," Ma said, "for Lamar a feast, too. We'd be eatin' on it for a week otherwise."

"Thank you, Ma." Arvilla's lips trembled between smiles and tears as she wrapped the young'uns up to go. "I—I wish I could stay."

And then she was gone, with Pa helping tote the children down the lane ready for Cousin George. Arvilla was tenderly carrying Silvy's gemstone picture done up in an old pillow slip.

"I aim to play my dulcimer some," Pa said when he came stomping back up the hill, "in case anybody but me's of a mind to sing."

Ma wiped her hands on her apron.

"I guess I could," she said. "Anything special you had in mind?"

" 'Blue Eyed Ellen,' for one." Pa sat down with his old cherrywood dulcimer and plucked a plaintive tune with a hickory pick. Silvy sat still as a mouse while Ma and Pa sang, with Granny's quavering voice joining in on "Sourwood Mountain" and "The Two Sisters."

"Do you call to mind a piece called 'Greenwillow Fair'?" Ma asked.

"I do," said Pa. "You sing the first part. I disremember some of the words."

Ma's voice rose high and sweet.

"I went to the fair without silver or gold,
My thoughts they were sad and my heart it was cold."

Silvy stared out at the snowy mountains. Sitting safe at home with the music rippling around her, she was near enough happy so it didn't matter.

"Greenwillow Fair, Greenwillow Fair,
I looked for my true love, my true love was there."

153

There was a rustle of sound at the back porch, and a shadow slanted across the snow for a second and disappeared. Silvy darted outside just in time to see Kel hurrying through the trees.

"Kel!" she called. "Are you passing by on Christmas Day and never even stepping inside?"

He came back slow-footed, with his head down.

"I thought—" he mumbled. "Clate thought—" Silvy noticed a slim white box beside the door. "Just a—"

Shivering in the cold, Silvy lifted a teardrop pendant of amethyst shading from near white to a deep violet like the shadows that were beginning to creep across the snow.

"Why, Kel! It's beautiful!"

Behind her the door opened.

"You'll be wearin' an onion poultice if you catch one of them chest colds," Granny said, "and us about out of onions." She passed Silvy her warm jacket. "I wish you a happy Christmas, Kelsey."

"Thank you, ma'am, and I wish you the same."

*"The sun shone like gold, and his smile warmed my heart.
Oh, I and my true love, we never will part."*

The music drifted out from the open door.

*"We came home happy from Greenwillow Fair,
With silvery moonbeams twined in my hair."*

Silvy clasped the pendant's thin gold chain around her neck.

"I do thank you," she told Kel. "I never ever had anything so pretty."

She wasn't about to take away from his gift by saying that, just now, like a flash of lightning, she had finally had an idea for her program at school.

"That's what I'll do. I'll set up a still in the gymnasium."
Lud skidded on the seat as the school bus swooped around
a curve that didn't look icy but was.

"You'll do no such of a thing!" Silvy said.

"Just a little one, and I won't run nothin' through it.
How'm I goin' to show the folks what all we use corn for
without a still?"

Some days Silvy wondered whether the Appalachian
Studies class wasn't getting a little too accurate about the
program she was getting up to illustrate what she and the
others were studying. She might just maybe have bitten off
more than she could chew when she had caught hold of
the idea on Christmas Day.

"How absolutely fabulous!" Jan had said when Silvy told her about her plans for the program that had been plaguing her all fall.

Jan had come out the last Saturday before school opened again to try out her Christmas skis before she went up to the slopes on Blue Mountain.

"Where I'll fall on my face." She had leaned the shining skis against the sales cabin. "I'll get an OK from the principal for the program so you can get started."

"I want to call it Greenwillow Fair." Jan had given Silvy a puzzled look. "After an old ballad that gave me the idea."

Since then the whole thing had grown bigger and bigger, like a twenty-five-cent balloon. Silvy just hoped it wouldn't blow up with a loud bang the way balloons lots of times did. Now the fair was going to be in April when the weather would maybe have settled and on a Saturday so the public could come, too, and stay however long they wanted. The way things stood now, it wasn't an assembly program at all, but Silvy would get credit for doing more than anybody else had.

"But you'll every one have to help out," Silvy had told the mountain kids. "We can't have these townies outdoing us."

Everybody got busy right then, with Miss Henderson joining in, too.

"I could consider using the fair as a substitute for your final examination if you do well with it," she had promised—just another reason why the class was going all out on the project.

The bus squealed to a stop at Lud's getting-off place, but he was still wrangling about the still.

"Cousin Sam'll help me if he gets out of the jailhouse in time and ain't too busy gettin' even with whoever turned him in. I was over to carry him a cake for Christmas and to get some pointers. Sam's sort of weak in the head, but he sure knows how to set up a still."

"No still!" Silvy repeated. "You'd get us all tossed out of school."

"I'll bring a hog then." Nothing could get the best of Lud for long. "It'd fit right in. Hogs eat corn, and maybe I could borrow a side of bacon somewhere to show if ours is all gone. That's corn twice removed."

"That'll be great!" said Silvy before he thought of anything worse.

Sometimes she woke up in the middle of the night, checking over in her mind what everybody had promised to do for the fair. Addie May was going to get her mother to set up one of her small-sized looms in the gymnasium and come and weave on it, too. Mary Ellerbe would bring an exhibit of the roots and herbs her family collected for the botanical company in town, with some old-time receipts for cough syrup and healing balm—not any that Granny didn't know, though.

By then, too, there might be wild flowers in bloom and some of the blossoming trees that Silvy could collect to show, Mary Ellerbe not being interested in flowers unless they grew on herbs. Silvy was planning to show her own kind of flowers, too, gemstone pictures to put alongside Kel's mineral display, which would be all about the rare earths he was so keen on.

"Might as well come out with everything I know," he said. "Doesn't look like anybody over at Highcliff or anywhere else is interested in what I'm doing."

It wasn't like Kel to talk discouraged, but Silvy didn't know that she blamed him. Likely she ought to feel discouraged herself, seeing neither one of them had heard a word about whether they were going to get the scholarships they had put in for. The truth was that Silvy hadn't had time to worry much. She was busy persuading Pa to

send some of his chairs for display and maybe even a dulcimer, and urging Ma to start a new quilt.

"I wish you'd make that hearts-bustin'-with-love pattern
you tried once before," Silvy said. "It was nigh the petti-
est ever.".

"I could," said Ma. "It'd be nice and bright to work on
in the wintertime."

"Pa," Silvy said, "I was wondering— Maybe you and
Ma would play the dulcimer and sing some."

Silvy wasn't overly hopeful about that, but it didn't hurt
to ask. Just as she had expected, Pa shook his head.

"I ain't gittin' out in a crowd of people to make mock of
myself," he said.

Then there was Clate to see, to find out if Silvy could
borrow some of his gemstones to show along with her and
Kel's display.

"You and Kel pick out whatever you want," Clate said.
"I might even come and look myself if Kel'll carry me to
town in the truck."

"I might," said Kel, "seeing it's your truck."

With all Silvy had to think about besides her usual
schoolwork, the winter went skittering by as fast as a
striped chipmunk running for cover with an acorn in his
cheek. On bright Saturdays when there wasn't too much
cold and snow, Silvy and Kel haunted the mine dumps
looking for pyrochlore and cyrtolite, the last on the list of
local minerals that were supposed to have Kel's rare earths
in them. Silvy, besides helping Kel, kept her eyes open for
material for Clate and for her own gemstone pictures.

"Gemflowers I'm going to call them," she told Clate,
who was a lot more interested than Kel was. "I wouldn't
doubt I can sell some of them when the tourists come
back."

"Wouldn't doubt you could," Clate agreed. "I could
handle some of them in my own shop, too, if you want.

Rock hounds'd be real taken with them. Tell you what I can do: I can order you whatever material you need—stones that we don't have around here—and you can pay me back whenever you sell the pictures."

"I thank you," Silvy said, "if you're sure—"

She didn't like for Clate to go to all that trouble, but she didn't like not having the right colors for her gemflowers either.

"You might fancy mosaic work whenever you got time on your hands." Clate rummaged around in the confusion of his shop and unearthed a tattered book. "This here helped me with my jewelry-making. Seems to me in the back chapter somewhere— Yeah, I got it, all about how to make mosaics. 'Tisn't easy, but I don't know what is, and you'd get a good price if you could ever put one together."

As far as Silvy could judge from a quick look, mosaic was a kind of inlay, mighty picky work, like the little box Pa had made once with a lot of different kinds of wood fixed in a pattern. Silvy's gemflowers were more like applique, something laid on canvas or burlap and fastened down. Already Clate was saving Silvy some broken bits and pieces of stones that weren't right for faceting or cabochon but that made nice flower petals or butterfly wings or ladybugs flying away home.

"I got no use for such as that," Clate said. "Save me the trouble of throwing them out."

Silvy suspected that he sometimes did give her pieces that he could use himself, but she couldn't prove it and didn't know that she wanted to try, pride or no pride.

"Givin's better than gittin'," Granny sometimes said. "Gives a body a heap of pleasure."

Still, Silvy'd like to pay Clate back some way. She had it in mind to put a little sign on whatever he sent to the fair, *Courtesy of Clate Fowler, Curiosity Cove,* so folks could go out to the cove and buy some of his pretties if they took a notion. She had already spread the word around school about where her amethyst pendant had come from, though mostly to Mary Ellerbe and others like her who wouldn't be big jewelry buyers. Jan, though, had taken notice, too.

"Does Mr. Fowler have them in other colors?" she asked.

"I guess. If he doesn't, he can make one up however you want."

Jan set down her transistor, tuned in to "Chain Around My Ankles, Fetters on My Soul," on the sunny steps of the school, where she and Silvy and a lot of others were getting a breath of air before it snowed again, which it was sure to do.

"My father said to ask you if you've heard anything out your way about somebody setting up an amusement park. The man was in the bank, and Daddy thought maybe your father would know."

"He knows, all right," Silvy said. "So far, the man's not having a drop of luck. He wanted to buy Pa out, but Pa's not selling."

Likely Mr. Colby wouldn't mind getting some interest money for his bank by making a loan to this Monteagle to set up Hillbilly Heaven. Silvy nearly gagged on the words. Mr. Colby had better not loan any of Silvy's savings— $37 and something now—for the project. If she thought he was going to, she'd step right down and snatch it out of the bank and put it away in Ma's old teapot.

"He's not selling? Why?" Jan asked.

"Pa's an ecologist," Silvy said smartly. That label would surprise Pa some if he heard it. "He's not about to let the —uh—environment get all polluted with something like that." That did sound impresssive, the result of looking at a lot of TV programs showing dead fish, soapsuds in the streams, and trees dying. "That's not to say there mightn't be others that'd fancy the idea."

"How's it going to pollute the environment?" Jan asked.

That stopped Silvy for only a minute.

"It isn't so much smoke and such. It's just junky. We got mighty little natural wilderness left in this country, and what we've got, it'd be nice to keep that way." Silvy felt pleased with herself, up to date as could be, and saying what she believed besides. "The man told Pa he was thinking about having a rock festival in the spring."

"He was?"

"Oh, my! Pa'd 've hit the ceiling if he hadn't been out in the open where there wasn't any."

"He and my father would have a lot in common," Jan said. "What's the matter with rock festivals?"

Drugs, from what Silvy had seen on TV. She eyed Jan narrowly. Probably she was talking the way she was just to be contrary, but—

"Oh, I'm not making the drug scene," Jan said.

"Never thought you were."

The fact was, she hadn't given drugs a thought, though she didn't doubt that the town kids went for them some. Right now that was their problem, not Silvy's. Townies seemed to fret about their identities and what a mess the world was in and how to have peace, which were all mighty important, but mountain folks couldn't get going on such high-level worrying until they had food on the table and clothes on their backs.

"What I get high on is rock music," Jan said. "It takes you out and away."

"You guarantee that? I've got a destination in mind."

"Well, actually, I guess not. You always have to come back in the end."

Silvy frowned as Jan went back in the building to the sound of "Weary Words, Sorry Song." It was too bad she couldn't latch onto something that'd keep her busy and interested. Silvy herself would be pleased to be a little less of both right now. Still, she wasn't ever bored, which Jan, unless Silvy misread the symptoms, pretty often was.

"What I'd give for the sight of something growing!" Granny grumbled one drippy day in February. "Seems it's been winter for a year and a half, and no hope of it ever changing. I got nothin' against evergreens and snow, but they've worn out their welcome with me."

"It won't be long now," Silvy said comfortingly. "Keep your mind on what's coming."

Maple, oak, and hickory would blossom pretty soon— not overly spectacular, but leading the way for the rest.

"Next month the serviceberry'll be out on the warm side of the slope." Granny cheered up a little. "My, oh, my, it looks like a snowdrift when it's all a-blossoming."

"Thought you were tired of snow," Silvy said. "Never mind, though. We'll go wild-flowering whenever the bloodroot and hepatica come out."

Then in April there'd be violets, Solomon seal, dogwood, trailing arbutus, and Silvy's name tree, the silverbell. In May— It seemed that every month of the year had flowers in a dozen different colors: pink laurel, flame azalea, rosy rhododendron, orange butterfly weed, blue lobelia, purple passion flower. Gemflowers for all seasons —the words popped into Silvy's head as though they had been waiting for her to open the door. What about making a different picture for each month or maybe more than one? The way she was doing them now, it'd be more a matter of color than accuracy, but if she got the hang of mosaic work, she could get in all the details by watching for just the right natural shadings in the stones. She'd have a good excuse to pleasure herself making the pictures because she'd be able to sell them and pay for her time and supplies.

The gemflower she was making now—not mosaic because she'd have to wait for summer to learn all the whys and wherefores of that—was hearts-bustin'-with-love, which Kel had suggested. Ma was making good progress on a quilt to match or anyway with the same reds in it. It could be she and Granny might want to do the same with some of the other gemflowers Silvy had in mind. Coordinated *decor*, which was what matching things were called in all the ads, might appeal to the tourists.

"I've written to Highcliff College," Miss Henderson announced the month before the fair, "urging them to send a representative or maybe more than one to look at the fair. Then, too, it will give whoever comes an opportunity to talk with at least two of you who are hoping to attend Highcliff next year. A personal interview is important."

Important for getting a scholarship, anyway. Silvy cast a discouraged glance in Kel's direction. She was going to be busy enough making sure everything was just right at the fair without trying to make a good impression on some professor that'd likely see right away that Silvy was no more an expert on rocks than a bird in a tree. Kel would do fine, though he wasn't by any means sure of that himself.

"I've got to find a specimen of cyrtolite by then," he said grimly, "so my exhibit'll be complete. I might have a little scrap of pyrochlore already—hard to tell for sure."

It was hard to identify a lot of the rare earth minerals, which had unsettling ways of looking like each other or something else entirely. By now, Kel had about given up trying to get Silvy all fired up about rare earths when it was really gemstones that fascinated her.

"They're rocks, too," she had told him once. "Think how outdone you'd be if I hated all rocks, from the least to the most."

Though she'd rather be spending what time she had on her gemflowers, she'd have to help Kel hunt for the cyrtolite every chance they had. She'd hate for him to miss his scholarship because he couldn't show everything he thought was needed.

"Cyrtolite's a source of yttrium, one of the important rare earth metals," Kel said, "and yttrium's used in a new method of making artificial diamonds that you can hardly tell from real. They grow the crystals out of a crucible of molten yttrium aluminum garnet."

"They do?" Once Silvy wouldn't have believed it if anybody had told her people could actually grow crystals, but if Kel said so it was bound to be true. "It'd be nice if you could grow you a few."

"It'd solve some problems, all right, like how to get to college."

He had ten times as good a chance as she did, as he well knew. Even without the cyrtolite he was fretting about, his exhibit for the fair was going to be so far ahead of everybody else's that nobody'd ever be able to catch up. He was planning on showing a sample of every local mineral he could find that was a source of the rare earths, and with them some of the products that used rare earths. So far his collection included a flashlight, a picture of an atomic reactor and another of a color TV, the flint from a cigarette lighter, some paint dryer, a magnet, a steel file, and a big piece of quartz that Clate had cut to look like one of the artificial diamonds Kel had been talking about.

"Just to show what one of them might look like," Kel said, "as an example of a use for yttrium."

The day before the fair everybody in the Appalachian Studies class was let loose in the gymnasium to set up the exhibits. A spinning wheel, a bear rug, one of Pa's chairs, some cornhusk dolls like Granny's, an old-time calico dress with a matching sunbonnet, some pottery and chinaware to show what feldspar was used for—the place was full of things tracing the past and the present.

Addie May and her ma were there, setting up the loom, all ready to weave in the morning. Silvy had her gemflowers and a couple of quilts that Ma and Granny had managed to get done to match up with the hearts-bustin'-with-love and the silverbell pictures. They were working on a dogwood pattern, all white and green, but they had given out of the green at the last minute, so Silvy had to be satisfied with just a pillow top of that. Kel, looking glum, was setting up his exhibit next to Silvy's.

"Looks real fine," she said.

"Could be better."

Silvy didn't take that much to heart. For Kel, even perfection wouldn't be quite good enough. Of course he was fretting about the scholarship man from Highcliff, as Silvy was, too.

"How're we going to know who he is?" she asked. "He might look us over and then go on home without ary a word."

"Could, though seems we could easy tell a professor from the folks around here."

Lud came thumping in from the parking lot with a big carton from which he unloaded a hickory-smoked ham, a side of bacon, a few ears of corn, some potatoes, a bag of cornmeal, a few jars of home-canned vegetables, and two heads of cabbage that must have been down in the root cellar all winter.

"Cousin Sam—he got out of jail last week already—he's bringing the hog in his truck first thing in the morning," he announced.

"You're never going to put that hog in the gymnasium!" Silvy said.

"I don't see why not. There's people been in here that ain't so much better'n hogs." He grinned at Silvy's expression. "Outside in the parking lot's where he's going to be, seeing you're all so high-toned. Pen's all set up beside the gym door with a trough and some straw for bedding. That suit you?"

The hog was better than a still, anyway, and Silvy

didn't doubt everybody that came would be real fascinated with one of the results of corn. All in all, it was going to be a pretty good display.

Even though Pa and Ma wouldn't come and sing, some of the class who were taking music were going to bring a dulcimer and sing some of the old songs, "Greenwillow Fair" included. It was all part of Miss Henderson's plan for mixing Appalachian Studies in with the regular school subjects. She hadn't had any field trips yet, but she had brought two people in to talk, a man from the Park Service and another whose father had been one of the first mountain doctors.

The sun was going down when Silvy and Kel started home in Clate's truck, borrowed for the day.

"Everything's as ready as it's going to be," Silvy said, close to being satisfied.

Going out of town, Lud passed them with a blast of the horn. Somebody sitting beside him stared from under a wide-brimmed felt hat.

"Cousin Sam, most likely," Silvy said.

"Not the genial type, I'd say, but maybe being in jail kind of curdles the disposition," Kel said. "Clate's coming in with us tomorrow—wants to see the exhibit and let the doctor take a look at his hip. He does seem to be walking some better."

Silvy nodded agreement. When Clate got all well and could go rock-hunting again, that'd be the end of the money Silvy and Kel would get for collecting gemstones for him—a mercenary thought that she swept out of her mind as fast as it came in.

"Is six-thirty too early tomorrow?" Kel asked.

"The sooner the better," said Silvy.

He and Clate picked her up so early that the road was still damp in the shadowy places that the sun hadn't reached yet. At school there wasn't a soul in sight. Silvy had to hunt up the janitor to let them into the gymnasium, bright with signs and fresh with some dogwood branches that Silvy had brought in the day before to prettify the place.

"Well, now," said Clate, "you got yourselves quite a display here."

"I'm proud of how everybody turned to and helped," Silvy said. "Take a look at what Kel's got set up. That professor's bound to give him a scholarship for that. He—"

She gave a horrified gasp. Kel's exhibit, so beautiful the night before, was a shambles. The signs were torn and crumpled, the flashlight was smashed on the floor, and Kel's precious minerals— Silvy stared at the wreckage.

"Half of them gone," she whispered, "and the rest strewn from here to yonder."

Kel just stood there, looking as though he'd been turned to stone.

"Now who'd do you thataway?" Silvy sputtered. "I'll find out, just see if I don't! And when I do—"

When she did, it'd be too late to do Kel any good. That exhibit meant everything to him—the hope of a scholarship, a college education, a chance to learn more about his intriguing minerals than he'd ever be able to find out for himself.

"We'll get it put together again," Silvy said, not really believing it.

"With my minerals lost? And the signs torn up?"

For the first time since Silvy had known him, Kel looked beaten down to nothing.

"We can't if we don't try," she said briskly. "Lucky we came early."

"Luckier if we'd come earlier still," Kel said. "We might have caught whoever did it."

" 'Might have' isn't going to get us a thing now." Silvy, against her nature, took charge, since Kel seemed completely fogged in. "First off, you better start gathering up every little bit of anything you can find on the floor, and Clate can help you sort it out."

Kel, mournful as a crow that had just been chased out of the cornfield, began picking up his crumpled signs and trying to locate the minerals that had been glued to them before whoever it was had ripped them off and tossed them every which way.

"Why'd they pick on me?" Kel asked. "I don't see where anybody else's exhibit was touched."

Silvy wondered about that herself. She couldn't think of a soul that'd have a grudge against Kel, though somebody must have. She'd seen on TV about people that liked to break things up just for the fun of it. If it was somebody like that, whoever it was could have had a lot better time ruining Silvy's exhibit or some of the others—pouring ink on Ma's quilts, for instance, or smashing the gemflower pictures or overturning Addie May's ma's loom and ripping out the weaving she'd set up on it.

"I'm going up to Miss Henderson's room and get some poster board for your new signs," Silvy said, "and let's hope—"

She let that sentence die—no use getting Kel any more upset than he already was by reminding him that if the professor from Highcliff showed up when the doors officially opened at nine o'clock, Kel would be just as badly off as he was right now. Heading for the hall, she heard Clate say, "The paint dryer's all spilled, but it looks like you could use the label off it for your exhibit or just the empty can, though somebody stomped down on it pretty hard."

When Silvy came back with the poster board and some marking pens, Kel was looking drearily at a few pieces of samarskite, euxenite, and uraninite he had found strewn around the gymnasium.

"He must have tossed the rest outside," Kel said, "or carried them off with him. That little smidgen of pyrochlore is gone, and the columbite and clarkeite and—"

"And cyrtolite, which you never had any of anyway," said Silvy, in no mood to listen to a recitation of what wasn't there.

"As for that busted-up flashlight," Clate said, "I've got one out in the truck that'll fill the bill. How about that quartz diamond I fixed up for you?"

"Gone," said Kel, "along with—"

"I'm going to hunt around some more places," Silvy said, "if you're sure you've looked everywhere in here."

"We have," said Clate. "Couldn't a mouse be hiding in this room and us not find it."

"You get busy on the new signs," Silvy said, "even if you don't have everything you need to go with them yet. You can always tell the professor what's supposed to be there. I'll be looking outside, and when Addie May and Lud come, they can help me hunt, too, if I can tear Lud away from that hog of his."

Surprisingly, the hog was in his pen just outside the gymnasium door, chomping away on some corn. Cousin Sam must have a light hand with hogs, to get this one unloaded and nobody hear a sound. Still, Kel and Silvy and Clate likely wouldn't have noticed if the roof had fallen in, taken up as they were with Kel's troubles.

Silvy eyed a truck standing in the far corner of the parking lot with a black felt hat, doubtless on Cousin Sam's head, looming up behind the wheel. She had half a notion to go and ask him to help her look for Kel's lost minerals, but she decided that from the little glimpse she'd caught of him going by in the car the night before, he wasn't the helpful type except maybe with relatives and hogs.

"We're here!" Addie May called as Lud's car pulled into the lot. "You and Kel must've left at sunup."

"Almost did." Silvy nodded howdy to Addie May's ma, who got out of the back seat and headed straight inside to her loom. "Listen, Addie May, something awful's happened! Somebody tore up Kel's exhibit!"

"Here's the hog already!" Lud didn't have eyes or ears for anything else. "Ain't he a whopper, though!" He turned to Silvy. "Where'd Cousin Sam go?"

"No place," Silvy said, "if that's him over yonder."

There was no use talking to Lud until he got through admiring the hog. Cousin Sam, tall and lean, got out of the truck and called to Lud in a hoarse voice.

"I got that hog parked real good for you, cousin," he said, sounding almighty pleased with himself. He yawned. "Came in town before first light to take care of a little chore, so all I got to do now is go see a feller that maybe's got some copper pipe I'm needin'. What time'll I come pick up the hog? Man over by Deer Lick Creek might buy it off me."

That voice, hoarse as a bullfrog's! Silvy had heard it somewhere a long while ago, though she didn't remember that face going with it or any other face, either. She—

"Hey!" she said. "You're him! The man that drove us off the bald with a rifle!"

"Don't seem likely, sissy."

He started to walk away, but Silvy ran after him, grabbing his sleeve.

"It *was* you!"

"What if it was? I got a right to go where I take a notion."

"I don't like rifles pointed at me. Pa'll take it unkindly when I—"

"Now, looky here. I got no quarrel with you or your pa, but ain't nobody going to get away with—"

A lot of Lud's chitchat that Silvy mostly didn't pay much attention to began to rearrange itself in her mind: "Figurin' out who turned him in . . . goin' to get even soon's he gets out of the jailhouse." Silvy got the message loud and clear like the detective in the Squad Car 97 show that was always having brainstorms at the last minute just before the villain got away.

"You worked it out that it was Kel turned you in! Only you didn't know who he was until you saw him in the truck going home last night and asked Lud. So you came back and—"

"I never! And even if I did, informers don't deserve no better!"

"He's not an informer! We didn't even know who you were or that you were blockading up there either!"

"Think I'm goin' to take your say-so? You just leave me be!"

"Sam, you listen here!" Lud's voice, for once, had a mean crackle to it. "If she says Kel didn't do it, he didn't. He don't care about ary a thing but rocks. Now what've you gone and done that you hadn't ought to?"

"Wrecked Kel's exhibit is what!" Silvy was close to tears. "Tore it all up and threw it out."

"He did?" Lud said. "Now, Silvy, don't you carry on! He'll put everything back."

"Who says?" Sam demanded.

"I say, for one!" Silvy said through her teeth, which were beginning to chatter. "You get all those minerals back and the other stuff, too, or I'll call the cops and you can go on back to jail before you're hardly used to being out."

"My, ain't you the little wildcat!"

"Yes, I am! Where're Kel's things? Quick, now!"

Cousin Sam gave up in the face of Silvy's anger and Lud's cold stare.

"Threw the most of 'em in the hog's pen afore I put him in. Maybe he's ate 'em by now!"

"He better hadn't!" Silvy was shaking, now that this particular war looked as though it was pretty much over.

Addie May, speechless until now, laid a soothing hand on Silvy's arm.

"Hogs don't hardly ever eat rocks," she said. "We'll get the things back."

"*He* will!" Silvy jerked a thumb in Cousin Sam's direction. "I never did root around in a hogpen and I'm not starting now!" Besides, she wasn't sure how long her knees were going to hold her up. It didn't come natural to her to fight with people, and it left her with a real quivery feeling. She managed to steady her voice. "Here's what's missing: a magnet, a steel file, some minerals, a piece of quartz cut to look like a diamond—"

Cousin Sam's eyes flickered, and Silvy pounced.

"Hand it here. That you wouldn't toss away."

Sam reluctantly dug into his jacket pocket and hauled out the quartz.

"I ain't envyin' whoever marries you," he mumbled. "Worst jawboner ever I heard!"

Addie May gave him a scorching look.

"You shut up!" she snapped. "Silvy, don't pay him any mind. Best if you go in and help Kel now. Lud and I'll take care of things out here."

Silvy couldn't resist a final reminder to Cousin Sam, just to polish things off.

"Yes, and don't forget those pictures you tore up. You head straight down to the TV store and get another picture of a color TV and—"

The photograph of the atomic reactor would be harder to come by, but maybe when Miss Henderson got here, she'd let Silvy into the library to look for another while Kel got the rest of his exhibit put back together. Time— that was what was fretting her. It must be pushing eight o'clock already, which wasn't any too long before nine, when goodness knew who might come walking through that door. Most of the Appalachian Studies class were here already, watching with grinning interest while Cousin Sam, grumbling, dug through the straw in the hog's pen. Lud tossed corn to the hog to keep it occupied.

"Ought to put on a few pounds by the time it gets out of here," he said, "with all the extra feed. Sam, you ain't looked under the straw in that far corner yet."

Leaving Addie May and Lud to see that Cousin Sam didn't skimp any on the looking, Silvy went back inside to pass the news to Kel and Clate and to take a last look at her own exhibit.

"We got him!" she said. "It was Lud's Cousin Sam who thought you turned him in for blockading that time up on the bald." Kel, feverishly lettering a sign that said *From Ancient Hills Comes Modern Technology*, looked up, bewildered. "Here's the quartz that I got back, and he's hunting for the rest of the stuff. He— Oh, well, I'll tell you all about it when you're not so busy. 'Tisn't exactly simple."

Kel stopped to give her a long look.

"Whatever you did, Silverbell," he said gently, "I thank you."

At nine o'clock when the doors opened to let in the first visitors, mostly school kids who crowded the entrance area, Kel had some of his exhibit put together and was working frantically on the rest. Lud and Addie May had brought in whatever minerals Cousin Sam had been able to retrieve, mixed in with dirt and straw and a scrap of plain old cement. Miss Henderson had hurried up to the school library herself and found a picture of an atomic reactor and had picked a magazine clipping of a color TV off the bulletin board.

"Saved you a trip downtown. Wasn't that nice?" Back out in the parking lot, Silvy spoke haughtily to Cousin Sam. He answered with a snort that she repaid with an angelic smile. "Now don't you feel better because you've done right?"

"Can't say I do," he said stubbornly. "Gotta start all over figurin' who it was that turned me in."

"Nobody, most likely," said Silvy. "Those revenuers get mighty smart some days. Don't you want to go along now before Kel catches sight of you?"

"You better had," Addie May said over Silvy's shoulder. "We got three men holding Kel down right now. He's just spoiling for a fight, and he'd sure make mincemeat of you, being twice as big and a heap younger."

"I'm a-goin'," Cousin Sam muttered, "but I'll be back for my hog before sundown."

Addie May stared cheerfully after his shambling figure.

"Nothing I love like a good fight," she said, "especially if my side wins."

They hadn't exactly won yet, but at least they were close to even, unless this professor from Highcliff came rushing in before Kel got his exhibit halfway back in shape.

"I better go see how Ma's doing," Addie May said. "Weaving that kiverlid's picky work, especially if folks keep throwing questions at her."

Silvy stood in the doorway for a minute to give a good all-over look at the fair. Lud had left off feeding the hog and stepped inside to the rest of his exhibit of home-grown stuff.

"It's thisaway," he was telling the principal. "Corn feeds

hogs and hogs make bacon, so I figure bacon's a sort of a byproduct of corn."

One of the musicians, sitting on a table with her legs hanging over, was plucking the dulcimer, and the other two were singing "Greenwillow Fair" while a crowd of visitors stood listening. Addie May's ma was weaving slow and steady. Mary Ellerbe had a bunch of leaves and herbs spread out to show, along with a dark concoction in a bottle that put Silvy in mind of one of Granny's cure-all mixtures. Over in the far corner, the kids from Misery Hollow that had taken history for their study had set up what was supposed to be an old-timey room, with a filled woodbox sitting next to an old cookstove, some rag rugs on the floor, and even somebody dressed up like an old granny-woman sitting in a rush-seated rocker with a clay pipe in her mouth.

"Not much different from how we live now." The granny-woman, choking slightly on the pipe smoke, winked under her sunbonnet at Silvy as she went by. "Townies don't know any better, though."

The only one that wasn't tending an exhibit was Silverbell Kershaw, and she'd better get with it. She slipped behind the table where her pictures were propped up in front of a sign, *Gemflowers for All Seasons*. Ma and Granny's quilts made a backdrop against the wall, and some of Clate's jewelry was spread out to show. Alongside, Kel and Clate were arranging their minerals in front of the signs that went with them.

"They looked better glued on," Kel mourned, "but on the whole they're not as bad as I thought. Nothing important's missing now except—" He glanced over at one of Silvy's gemflower pictures. "Where'd you get that bumblebee?"

"It was in a batch of stones Clate gave me out of the tumbler. Just the right shade of brown for a bumblebee."

Kel gave it a closer look.

"I've got a notion it's cyrtolite, or some of it is."

He got out his magnifying glass and looked again. Silvy's lips tightened. Hadn't she done enough already without having to give up that bumblebee, which was near about the best thing in the picture? But what if having the cyrtolite would make the difference between Kel's getting his scholarship and not getting it? Kel straightened up.

"You're sure that's what it is?" Clate asked in a mild voice. "Could be a honeystone."

"A honeystone? Never heard tell of—" He looked from Silvy to Clate and back again. "Well, now that you mention it— Anyway, it doesn't look just like cyrtolite —some other kind of zircon, most likely."

Silvy let out her breath again. It was hateful to be glad it wasn't cyrtolite, but it did save her from having to argue with herself about whether to give it up to Kel for his display.

"You can tell the professor when he comes that cyrtolite looks kind of like that," she said doubtfully.

She eyed the visitors that were working their way through the exhibit—a big crowd of town kids, which surprised Silvy a little, since mostly they never showed much interest in how things were back in the coves and hollows. Quite a few adults were coming now, and Silvy gave each one a good sharp look.

"Nary a one looks like a professor," she told Kel. "More like plain, ordinary folks. Look over yonder. That's Mrs. Colby talking to Addie May's ma. Jan must be around somewhere, too."

She was, over by the folk singers with a tape recorder, asking for this song or that song and taking a good look at the dulcimer. She waved her hand at Silvy but didn't budge from the spot. It would be a fine thing if Jan would take an interest in the old folk songs, either to sing them or collect them—something to aim for. Pa and Ma might even be coaxed to sing for her in private if Silvy happened to hit them in the right mood.

"Yes, ma'am?" Silvy had an audience of her own now, a couple of women in pants, rock hounds, most likely. "Why, thank you. I think they're pretty, too. Gemflowers for every time of the year, and the quilts to match that Ma and Granny make. No, ma'am, nothing's for sale here today—just on exhibit. No, ma'am, I don't do mosaics yet, but I'm going to learn this summer." She looked sideways at Kel's exhibit. She did wish somebody'd come and look at his besides the principal, who was inspecting everybody's, one after the other. The questions came flying at her as a few more people gathered. "This one's silverbell and that one yonder is hearts-bustin'-with-love that comes out so pretty in the fall, and dogwood at the end. I'm trying to get together enough stones for fringed phacelia, only I want to do the blue kind, and that shade is extra hard to come by."

A couple of men in uniform came in, one of them the Bob Sexton that had asked for Lud that time. Silvy gave an exasperated sigh as they stopped to speak to Lud. If he'd been acting up so the law was after him, she'd never forgive him, spoiling the fair that way. At least Silvy hadn't let him set up that still, even a make-believe one.

"You tell her!" Lud, grinning, yelled in Silvy's direction. "She don't believe it."

Bob Sexton edged his way to Silvy.

"Lud Bickett says I should tell you the Park Service really is going to set up a still along the parkway this summer—an authentic part of the history of the region, along with molasses making and cornmeal grinding. We've about talked Lud into helping us out on it."

"He'll do you a good job," Silvy said. Besides, he'd have expert advice from Cousin Sam and some of his other relations. Not only that, it might keep him from getting into trouble himself, which might be what Mr. Sexton had in mind. "He'll do what he says he'll do."

When folks trusted Lud, he'd never let them down, for all his big mouth. In the meantime, where was this professor that was going to talk to Kel and her? She gave Kel what she hoped was an encouraging glance, but he was busy talking to a man who looked as though he'd just come in from hunting rocks himself. Anyway, he'd be a good one for Kel to practice his explanation on to get it polished up before the professor came.

"Rare earths, h'm?" The man turned so Silvy got a good look at his face. It was funny how many folks were turning up today, like on Decoration Day when everybody came back from wherever they were to fix up the cemetery at Deer Lick Creek. This was the man she and Kel had met in Clate's lane, the one that had maybe followed them around that day or maybe hadn't—another land buyer, according to Clate. "You've got an interesting study here."

Another woman started asking Silvy a lot of questions then, but she could still catch a phrase now and then as Kel talked about those rare earths of his.

"Columbium for high-temperature aerospace alloys . . . lasers . . . activators for fluorescent lights . . . new artificial diamonds . . . samarium for control rods in nuclear fission . . ." He jerked his thumb toward Silvy's gemflowers. "That bumblebee's cyrtolite, one of the sources of yttrium."

So all of a sudden that bumblebee had turned from honeystone, whatever that was, into for-sure cyrtolite, unless— Maybe he'd just pretended it wasn't cyrtolite for fear she'd spoil her picture to help him out. Likely she would have, too, though maybe not. Sometimes she was as big a puzzle to herself as she could possibly be to anybody else. Kel's voice went on.

"Rare earths in the atmosphere, they think . . . could be

on the moon, along with the feldspar they found . . . minerals a million years old used in the new technology . . ."

Kel was a smart one, figuring out that minerals could be the jumping-off place from the past to the future—for him anyway. Maybe for her, too, if the gemflowers ever got her anything. She shifted wearily from one foot to the other as the hours passed. People came and went, she answered a million questions, give or take a few, Kel explained about the rare earths over and over, and still nary a professor had stuck his head in the door. If Silvy could have had her druthers, she'd go off in a corner somewhere and have a good cry, and from the looks of him Kel felt about the same.

"Closing time," Miss Henderson said. "It was a wonderful fair you planned, Silvy." Wonderful if only the professor had come to take a look. Otherwise, it was just something Silvy had worked out to prove mountain folks could do as well as anybody else—better, even. "Best of all, you and Kel made a favorable impression."

"On who—uh—whom?"

"Why, Professor Holloway from Highcliff and Mrs. Weston, who's in charge of the craft shops over there."

"Kel!" Silvy called. "Listen here! They came and never even *said!*" She turned back to Miss Henderson. "You mean we might get our scholarships?"

"They said they still have to check some things, but you'll hear for sure pretty soon."

All the way home in the truck, Kel and Silvy ranged from hope to despair and back again until Clate said, "Either you'll get 'em or you won't. 'Twon't help any to work yourselves into a froth."

Silvy ignored that.

"I'm already in one, too deep to get out! Kel, it could have been—"

"Could have been anybody," Kel said. "I didn't see anyone that had *Professor* painted on his forehead. What was it Miss Henderson said? Holloway and Weston?" He stopped at the foot of Silvy's lane. "I'll help carry your things up to the house."

"Unload them at the cabin down here, why don't you? Pa can give me a hand soon's he gets through talking to—"

Here he was again, the man that had been in Clate's lane and at the fair, too, looking at Kel's rocks. Pa's voice rose.

"I already told this partner of yourn I ain't goin' to sell one inch of my land for no Hillbilly Heaven or any other thing whatsoever. No, sir, Holloway! No's my last word, and I don't want to hear no more about it."

Holloway! It was Professor Holloway from Highcliff that Pa was roaring at like a wounded bear raring up on his hind legs to defy a hunter.

"Best take the things to Clate's for now," Silvy said through tears, and stumbled up the lane toward home.

It was good-bye, scholarship, for extra sure this time.

"'Tisn't right!" Silvy stared at a slope covered so thickly with blossoming silverbell that hardly a speck of green showed through—just clouds of white touched ever so faintly with pink. "Just because Pa did me out of my scholarship by talking so hateful to that Professor Holloway, it's no reason he should be mad at you, too."

"I don't think that had a thing to do with it." For once Kel, sitting on a rock outcropping, wasn't looking to see what it was made of. "There's a world of people want scholarships, and likely I just didn't measure up."

More likely Silvy was the one that hadn't measured up, Pa or no Pa.

"Besides," she said, hope sounding better than despair any day, "it hasn't been but three weeks."

And seemed like three years, what with all her fuming and fretting and hashing everything over a dozen times. She took another look at the blossoming trees, which should have cheered her up but didn't. Anyway, the scenery was pretty around here—a good thing, seeing she'd likely be looking at it for a good long while. Maybe if she stuck to peddling gemflower pictures and quilts and cornhusk dolls for ten years or so, she'd get enough saved up to go to Highcliff by the time it was too late to matter. More likely, she'd just give up after a while, marry somebody she didn't care a lot about, and end up like Arvilla, no better off than when she started.

"What I hate, too," she said, "is that Mr. Holloway would be tied up with that Hillbilly Heaven man. It doesn't seem right for a professor."

"Could be your pa was mistaken," Kel said, "seeing he was so riled up already about that other man that came asking."

Whether he was mistaken or not, the harm was done, the professor gone away, probably mad as a hornet, and Silvy's scholarship gone with him—not that Pa had said ary a word on the subject when he came up to the house again. He had just gone into the shed and started playing "Barbara Allen" on the dulcimer, doleful as could be.

"I take it kindly of Lud to go against his own kin and make Cousin Sam root around after my things," Kel turned around to catch the sun on his face. "I told him so, too."

Silvy had done the same, one day when Lud had come over to borrow Pa's ax.

"Who said I was doing it for Kel? It was for you," he had blurted. "Couldn't stand you feeling so bad." He had kicked at an innocent piece of firewood beside the house. "I guess you wouldn't want to—uh—take up with—"

Silvy could have cried. For all Lud was so loud-mouthed

and oafish lots of times, he had feelings, the same as anybody else.

"Lud, Addie May's real proud of your job you got with the Park Service, no matter how she talks sometimes. Couldn't you—"

"She is?" A new idea, from his expression. "Addie May's OK. She got that doll for me that your granny made to look like you." He had studied her face. "You ain't mad?"

Not mad, just sorry that Lud had a dream that wasn't going to come true either—a real common trouble around here.

"We better get on over to the mine dump," she told Kel now. "We won't find any rocks around here."

"Who cares?" Kel said. "Rocks'll be here when the flowers are long gone."

"Yes, but—" That was a turnaround if Silvy had ever seen one. "Clate needs some golden beryl the worst way."

And Kel needed to hunt rocks, no matter what else might be going to happen. If he stopped, it'd be like giving up without a fight.

"Hush your noise, Bugle! Ain't no bear up here!" Pa was threading his way through the rhododendron, with the dogs fanning out around him. He turned to speak to somebody following along back among the bushes. "Ain't this a sightly spot now? Can't even see anybody's chimney smoke from up here." Old Blue, tail wagging, headed for Silvy. "You did give me a start, Silverbell, popping up out of nowhere thataway. And Kelsey."

"You were the one that popped," Silvy said. "We were here already."

Pa beckoned his lagging companion on.

"'Tain't easy goin', Holloway, but it's worth the climb."

Professor Holloway finally made it as Kel and Silvy stared, downright stupid from astonishment. One day Pa was blasting Mr. Holloway off the place, and now he was showing him around, polite as could be.

"This here's Kelsey McLeod," Pa said, "that lives over yonder. And my least young'un, Silverbell."

Mr. Holloway shook hands with Kel and nodded to Silvy.

"Glad to see you again," he said, but right away he turned to look at the view—the frothy white slope and behind it the bluey-green mountains rolling away to the end of beyond.

"You're acquainted already?" Pa said.

Silvy nodded. How could she tell Pa about the lost scholarship with the professor standing right there within earshot?

"Beautiful!" Mr. Holloway eyed the rock outcropping that Kel had been sitting on. "Anything interesting here?"

"Just pegmatite," Kel said, "with nothing special in it that I can see, but Silvy found some zoisite down by Mr. Kershaw's barn, and I figure there ought to be some more around here if there was any way to get at it. Take a look at that over yonder. I got a notion it could be—"

"Pa!" Silvy whispered. "What's going on?"

"Nothin'," Pa said. "This Holloway's lookin' for somewhere to stay summers and weekends where nobody'll bother him while he studies about rocks, same as Kel. Fixin' to write a book about 'em, he says."

"But, Pa, he's—"

"No, he ain't! Hasn't got ary a thing to do with that Hillbilly Heaven!" Pa looked sheepish. "I ain't sellin' any land to him or anybody else, but I talked so rough to him first time around that I figured I'd do him a favor and show him some of our scenery to make up."

"Silvy and I are going over to the mine dump now," Kel said diffidently to the professor. "If you'd want to come, you're welcome."

Kel being so polite must make Mr. Holloway feel guilty about not giving him the scholarship, though likely he didn't have all the say-so about it anyway.

"I'll take a rain check," the professor said. "I came over on business." He smiled. "Could have handled it by mail before now, but any excuse to visit this area is a good one for me."

"We'll be going along then." Kel lifted a hand in farewell. "Pleased to have seen you again."

"Wait a minute! This business is with you. I brought over your scholarship papers."

"You mean we got 'em?" Silvy wasn't really surprised about Kel, but she had to be certain sure about herself. "The both of us?"

"Right. Mrs. Weston will want you to put your work hours in on gemflowers and mosaics for sale in the craft shop—something different for the customers."

"Oh, my!" Earning her way by doing what she liked to do was almost too good to be true. "I do thank you, more than I can say."

Pa looked from one to the next.

"This here's a professor from that place you want to go to school at?" He gave Mr. Holloway a studying look. "And you never said."

"Well, no. If I had, and you had let me buy a piece of your land, it might have been misinterpreted—sell me the land or I won't give Silverbell the scholarship—though it's a committee that passes on the scholarship grants, not just one person."

"Seems there's a lot goin' on that nobody told me about," Pa said. "Didn't even know Silverbell had asked for one of these scholarships. Hold on, though! Kershaws ain't never taken charity, from colleges or the government or the welfare or—"

"Oh, Pa! It's not charity! It's a scholarship for knowing how to make my gemflower pictures."

"She'll be doing us a favor," Professor Holloway put in, smooth as a gallon of honey. "The college earns a sizable amount by making mountain things to sell to the visitors."

"Then you do your best, Silvy," Pa said, "so's not to be beholden. Only now I don't know but it's me that's beholden."

Professor Holloway turned to Kel.

"I'll want you in my own department to help run tests on some of the local minerals and do some more investigation on the rare earths and their local application, if any."

Silvy looked at Kel. That made two of them in heaven or mighty near it.

"I'll meet you down at the road," the professor said, "and give you the papers."

He and Pa and the dogs headed toward home.

"You're welcome to come out any time," Pa said. "Latchstring's always out. I might even throw you up a little cabin sometime, just to keep my hand in, if—"

Silvy hung back for a last look at her name flower, fluttering in a little breeze. Here she was, about to step out into tomorrow, just the way she'd hoped, but she was already homesick before she'd even left and mighty scared besides. Kel reached for her hand as they turned to follow Pa and the professor.

"Highcliff's going to be mighty different from here," he said in a muffled voice. Why, he was as shook up as Silvy, from the looks. "We'll have to kind of hang together."

"Yes," said Silvy, "we will, but between the two of us, I don't doubt we can handle just about anything."

Being raised around here made folks sturdy as a pine tree. Besides, wherever she and Kel went and however long they stayed away, they'd still be rooted good and solid in the mountains like rosebay rhododendron growing the hard way in a wilderness of rocks.